D1331697

Windsor and Maidenhead

9580000182510

NO TOUCHING

Ketty Rouf

NO TOUCHING

*Translated from the French
by Tina Kover*

Europa
editions

Europa Editions
8 Blackstock Mews
London N4 2BT
www.europaeditions.co.uk

This book is a work of fiction. Any references to historical events,
real people, or real locales are used fictitiously.

Copyright © Editions Albin Michel – Paris 2020
First Publication 2021 by Europa Editions

Translation by Tina Kover
Original title: *On ne touche pas*
Translation copyright © 2021 by Europa Editions

All rights reserved, including the right of reproduction
in whole or in part in any form.

A catalogue record for this title is available from the British Library
ISBN 978-1-78770-316-2

Rouf, Ketty
No Touching

Book design by Emanuele Ragnisco
www.mekkanografici.com

Cover photo © Kseniya Ovchinnikova / Getty Images

Prepress by Grafica Punto Print – Rome

Printed and bound in Great Britain by Clays Ltd, Elcograf S.p.A.

CONTENTS

NO TOUCHING

PART ONE
I DANCE, THEREFORE I AM

Today, I don't exist.

Tomorrow, I probably won't, either.

This weekend, I'll knock back a few Diabolo mint citron sodas on my own. I'll lick my fingers, all of them, after scarfing down some peanuts.

I look down. The graveled concrete slabs wink at me. They sparkle like the sand crystals in playground asphalt. I line my feet up on the crack between two slabs and then jump with both feet. My own personal game of hopscotch.

At this rate, I'll miss the bus.

I really couldn't care less.

Today is the first day of school.

I know the five-thirty A.M. sidewalks by heart, the bus stops, the crosswalks, the metro with its anti-slip strips on the platforms. This is my Way of the Cross: five bus stops, forty minutes on the metro, two changes, seven minutes' walk, another station, thirty-five minutes on the train. On the bus, and the metro, and the train, and sometimes even while walking, I read erotic novels. Last year I got through *The She Devils*, *Thérèse the Philosopher*, *The Solar Anus*, *The Story of O*, and *Punishment of a Cock*. Two hours of eroticism, paper-and-ink-style: pages and pages of filthy language that I flip through the way you reel off a rosary, my prayer at each station before the Calvary of the high school. Today, I slipped a volume of Apollinaire into my bag, thinking that starting the year off with a masterpiece might help me get going. "He squeezed those regal buttocks and had inserted his index finger into an arsehole of exquisite tightness." The poet's prose is better than the fresh-squeezed orange juice and vitamins I had at breakfast. But the book slips out of my hands; it's impossible to read when your eyes are full of tears. *The Eleven Thousand Rods* will have to wait.

The aluminum gates are in exactly the same place as last year, staring at me from their thick gray bulk. I look down; it creeps me out, this Alcatraz. How many times have I imagined myself backing up, turning around, walking away forever? I don't dare calculate the amount of time I've already spent here, or the number of times I've asked for a transfer. Every year I feel like I'm acting in the same movie—or perhaps I should say the same scene is playing me. This year is no exception: same building, same colleagues, same inevitable chaos, same three classes, same syllabus. I stop walking. One, two, three, four . . . I start moving again, I must. I press the button to be buzzed in, but the gate doesn't open. The janitor's voice crackles through the speaker, telling me to push. I force the heavy gate open with difficulty.

"Oh, hi, Joséphine . . . You're late, too!"

Madame Louis, the math teacher, has looked back at the screech of the gate. I lengthen my stride as she moves slowly toward the front door. I look down. I have no desire to see the concrete expanse of this place again, the graffiti-covered benches, the central hub of the building with its two wings, the endless rows of identical windows stretching away on each side. Like huge pincers ready to crush the air. I prefer to focus on my sequined ballerina flats, keeping rhythm. "Slide, slide, slide, Madam Slug. Slide, slide, slide, Mister Snail."

The teachers' lounge smells like bad coffee and cheap after-shave. Nausea grips me. Some of my colleagues are hanging out here; others, more disciplined, are undoubtedly in the meeting room already, waiting for the principal's welcome-back speech. I don't want to talk. I can feel my voice deserting me, my jaw clenching in a forced smile. The same smile, I'm sure, that I can see on some of the faces around me. What a mess. It's like they're hung over but without having partied. They're as drab as their clothes: gray spots and faded brown. Do I look as lifeless as that? The only face I've been looking forward to seeing just smiled at me. Martin pulls me out of my dreary reverie by giving me a hug. He teaches French and is the only friend I have in the school.

We find seats in the very back row of the meeting room. The principal starts his long-winded spiel.

"I want to thank you for your hard work last year; an 89.9%

average on the baccalaureate exam is a job well done. Our school's been given a good ranking because of it; we've moved ahead of André-Malraux. You know how important our reputation is to me . . ."

I pretend to raise my little finger, like I want to say something. That makes Martin smile.

"But I'm sure we can aim even higher. This year I want to see perfect scores. And I know you'll do whatever needs to be done for every student to pass the *bac*."

The sound of rustling and soft, stifled laughter ripples through the room. Martin's face darkens and he looks down. I nudge him with an elbow and whisper in his ear, low:

"If I may affirm my personal creed . . . I believe in the all-powerful average, like student X, who achieved the miraculous result of graduating with a 20.3 out of 20. I even believe that, this year, we can have more graduates than we have students."

I love imitating the principal, and Martin thinks it's funny too. It's my way of making things less miserable. I feel a little stronger when I'm with him. Brave, even, sometimes. But today, my body isn't helping me at all. I make a dash for the exit, a tissue pressed to my mouth. My stomach turns over. I head for the bathroom. To vomit, or shit, or read Apollinaire—anything but listen to that speech in the stilted language of the Ministry of National Education. I need to calm down. I think ahead to when I'll start to feel better. In a few hours I'll be back home with my new scented candles, corset laid out on the bed, stockings tucked away in a dresser drawer, high heels on the bedside table. It makes me feel better to think of the moment when, dressed in black lace and stilettos, I'll swallow a Xanax, or two. One more day forgotten in a haze of lingerie and benzodiazepines. For now, though, there's nothing but my exhaustion. I only slept a few hours last night. The anxiety of the new school year, made longer by a dream, was stronger than the Xanax. A nude dancer was swaying her hips onstage and I, the only woman in an all-male audience, was drinking champagne and watching her dance. I orgasmed as I slept, and the pleasure woke me, along with the need to pee.

I emerge from the bathroom.

I don't know where I am anymore.

I fainted right in the midst of my colleagues, who had gathered for the general meeting. I went down like a ton of bricks, knocking over two or three chairs. Caused quite a commotion. Spectacular, according to Martin. That's me, the heroine of back-to-school prep day: low blood pressure. Fainting. Ambulance. Sick leave.

The body falters but refuses to give way. I'm a philosophy teacher. I resist. That's what philosophy is for: objecting to the idea that our existence is a pointless exercise in exhaustion. And I know what I'm talking about; I've been marinating in it forever. It started when I was a kid and would visit our neighbor, a university professor who'd never had children. Three times a week, at around five o'clock, I tasted the delights of philosophy with her. At eight years old, existence and metaphysics tasted like hot chocolate and Petit Beurre shortbread.

My doctor prescribed medical leave without batting an eyelash, told me to stop taking beta-blockers and avoid sad things.

"Number one, beta-blockers are the only thing that keeps my migraines away, and number two, my whole life is sad, almost."

"Maybe you should think about talking to someone."

"Talking to someone? About something so small?"

I hadn't even finished the sentence when my eyes began spurting fat tears. I couldn't stop. I stayed in his office for a good hour.

Something so small? God, what a loser I am! All these

"small" things that make up my life are turning into a real dumpster fire, and fast. How have I ended up such a hopeless mess? No recognition, no money, no happiness. And the unbelievable idiocy of having decided to be a teacher. Seduced by a bunch of pretty talk about values, I let myself get fucked by the illusion that I was carrying out some noble mission. *Educating people, what a wonderful profession.* And the vacations. Vacations I usually spend working, and never too far from home.

See, I always fall into the same trap. Asking myself questions that bring up other questions, and always lead to a complicated answer, never a simple yes or no. In philosophy, we call that a problematic. But there will be no dissertation today, because the days to come are stretching out in front of me with their parade of promises: nights without insomnia, waking up without crying, actually being able to digest food. Happiness, as simple as a healthy body.

The doctor was sympathetic. I've got a whole six days of sick leave ahead of me.

It started raining, and I didn't have an umbrella. That's why I went inside. I stepped through the curtain of light, walked down the red carpet, and paid a hundred and twenty-five euros, with a free bottle of champagne thrown in. Screw getting caught, and the hangover. That was nine months ago, the last day of summer vacation. At ten minutes to midnight, sitting in a plush seat at 12, avenue George V, I slipped into a dream. The dancer onstage was naked, swiveling her hips. Slightly more swaybacked than the others, her head held high, she winked naughtily at a man in the audience. Her lipstick was blood red. A string of pearls hung between her ass cheeks.

That night, the real world ceased to exist. I felt *alive*. Ever since then, when even the Xanax won't put me to sleep, I go out very late instead of lying in bed. I roam around Paris with no goal except losing myself. No watch, no phone. The only destination that matters to me is the underground place of my absence. I wander the streets at random, and the next day, drunk with fatigue, I hurt a little less. I can't think about anything but sleep. It takes urgent, overriding needs to make the pain go silent.

Last night I spent another hundred and twenty-five euros, drank another bottle of champagne, watched the same show. The desire to see the dancer came back like a need, magnified by the night into a dream. She's still there, onstage, in her all-powerful nakedness. I envy her desperately. Not just her body,

though I'd love to know what it's like to have a perfect body. I
envy her because she's nude. Perfectly nude. I compare myself
to her, just for fun: I may not have a smile like hers, but I have
the right lipstick, that red that makes you a woman, Rouge
Dior No. 999. I bought it, even though I'll never wear it. The
pleasure of owning it is just as deep as my qualms about wearing a red that intense. Teachers don't buy Christian Dior cos-
metics. They're too expensive. The red is too red. To give
myself the courage to wear it, I signed up for a trial lesson at
a striptease school I found by chance. That "chance" that
doesn't exist. You can hold a master's degree in philosophy,
and have cellulite and stretch marks, and dream of being a
nude dancer. You have to cling to something, and what better
to cling to than yourself? The body is weightier than an idea.
The dance class was exactly how I imagined it would be: really
interesting, but it didn't encourage you to continue. It's hard to
love your body. I signed up for a year's worth of classes.

At first, I ignored the huge mirror in the studio. But being
there, right in front of a mirror I couldn't muster up the
courage to look at myself in, it was unavoidable. I started out
by focusing on individual parts of my body. First, the ankles.
Then the eyes—the gaze is the most important thing. And last,
my cleavage. A good chunk of my meager savings went into
Cellu M6 treatments, and my embarrassment started to vanish
along with the cellulite. One day, I looked straight into the mirror. I watched a foot in a red stiletto sketch a *rond de jambe* and
come to rest elegantly on a chair, a pair of breasts tilt toward a
thigh sheathed in black fishnet stockings, a hand sliding along
it with still-timid grace. The foot, the breasts, the thigh . . . they
were mine. I left the studio. In the changing room, my whole
body trembled. I let it. Tears made little black circles beneath
my lightly mascaraed eyes.

Every week, I wait eagerly for Friday evening at 6:30. An hour
and a half when I feel alive. So a student spat on the doorknob

that I was the first one to turn? I cling to my boa; its feathers will be my wings. The youngest girl in my class called me a fucking whore? I learn to make my nipple-tassels spin in circles. The principal refused to convene a meeting of the disciplinary committee? I buy new stockings that I'll wear at home, in my kitchen, in bed.

Last week, I was accepted into the dance school's intermediate level. This is where you learn to dance in twelve-centimeter stilettos. As I was jotting down the address of a high-heeled shoe store from one of the school bulletin boards, my gaze fell on a glossy-haired brunette whose green eyes were fixed on me as she fingered the shoulder-strap of her push-up bra. Her scarlet lips whispered in my ear: "Want to become a dancer at Dreams, Paris's hottest club for striptease *à la française*? If you're a beginner, we provide high-quality training for free. Auditions every Saturday (by appointment). For more information or to book an appointment, call Andrea at 06 12 18 76 95. Please bring a pair of high heels, lingerie, and a robe to auditions."

Along with the shoe store's address, I tucked Andrea's number into my bag.

P hilosophy's pointless, Madame."
I'm setting my books down on the desk when Hadrien's
voice rises from the last row in the classroom on the left.
I unbutton the right sleeve of my blouse and pick up my pen.
The coursework log is empty. I look up at the thirty-three stu-
dents in senior class L.

"What year is it?"

I know September is over, and it's only my third week back
at the high school after sick leave, but already I'm having trouble remembering the date and even the year. Something is
blurring my perception of time, like a thick sheet of bubble-
wrap separating me from the world.

"It's 2005, Madame."

Hadrien has a teasing smile on his face. He's the brightest
and the most inconsistent student I've ever had. A young man
of seventeen, stagnating in that part of life Kierkegaard called
the "aesthetic stage, living only in the present and, conse-
quently, doomed to despair." Hadrien can recite passages from
Nietzsche's *Beyond Good and Evil* from memory, like an actor
playing to his audience, and sometimes he relieves the boredom of hours spent in the classroom by trying to control the
tone of the burps he emits in the direction of the window.
Exuberance clings to him like a second skin. Exhaustion, too.

I've enjoyed watching him ever since he became my student. He's become my distraction here at school. I imagine him
losing his youth somewhere in a beer glass and rediscovering it

on the football field, launching himself wildly at the goal. He's a good attacking midfielder, according to my colleague in Phys Ed. The class responds to his charisma, but Hadrien isn't a leader. Just a boy with talents to be used for good or evil. I often notice him squirming in his seat, gazing absently at his notebook with its torn-out pages, the end of his pen chewed like a piece of gum.

"Philosophy's pointless, Madame."

"Very good, Hadrien; you've been studying. I'm honored, and I don't mean that sarcastically."

The other students, surprised at first, come noisily to life, tossing questions at me like rocks, about the usefulness of any of it: the *bac*, the student councils, the nicotine and suffering. I decide not to try to control the barrage of questions and write the date in the coursework log. My eyes stray toward the door. What if I just walked out? The students aren't even looking at me, too absorbed in their desire to do nothing. I wonder if I exist.

"Philosophy's such a headache . . ."

"This stuff doesn't accomplish anything . . ."

"Madame? Madame, my stomach hurts. Can I go and see the nurse?"

"Philosophers are nutjobs . . ."

"Can I go to the bathroom, Madame? I've gotta piss!"

"We're never going to earn a living from philosophy . . ."

I start trying to shout them down.

Is it even possible to shout louder than them?

It's ten o'clock in the morning, and I'm already wiped out. My eyes are prickling, and I'm sure I'm going to cry.

"Cut it out, you assholes, you're pissing her off!"

Silence falls at the sound of Hadrien's voice. A wave of excited tittering sweeps the room. They'll listen to me for at least fifteen minutes now; better rise to the occasion, swallow my tears and tell them about Diogenes, the madman who lived

naked in a barrel and walked around barking like a dog, uri-
nating and masturbating in public. The body—that gets their
attention, especially the naked part. I seize the opportunity to
introduce the discourse on the quest for virtue. Starting out
with something concrete is always a good way to ease into a
subject, it's their personal philosophy. They aren't wrong,
really.

Half an hour later, saved by the bell, I linger in the classroom. A bit of sweetness has found its way into the chaos of my
thoughts. I take the gift I found in my pigeonhole this morning
out of my briefcase.

"How goes it, *Madame la philosophe*?"

Martin's smile detaches itself from the door frame and
brings me back to reality.

"Fine, and in a few hours it'll be a whole lot better."

"Want a coffee?"

"No sugar, thanks. And that's two thank yous I owe you,
actually. You remembered. I loved finding it in my pigeonhole—nice change from administrative memos."

"Like a waft of sweet perfume amid the dusty smells of
duty? I'm sure you're going to love it."

We head for the cafeteria. Martin's given me Pierre
Michon's *Rimbaud the Son*. We keep our literary marriage alive
with the devotion of young newlyweds. Every month we give
each other a book, or a collection of poems.

I noticed him as soon as he started at the school—two
years, it's been, already. Like me, he kept his distance from
everyone else, concentrating on a book or busily making
copies. Some colleagues took him for a snob, another intellectual determined to guard his ivory tower built of culture and
self-importance. One day I found a sheet of paper he'd forgotten near the photocopier: "I am the Dark One,—the
Widower,—the Unconsoled, / The Aquitaine Prince whose
Tower is destroyed . . ." When Martin came back to the empty

computer lab at five o'clock to get the forgotten page, I was there, holding it.

"Gérard de Nerval, 'El Desdichado.' 'My forehead is still red from the Queen's kiss.' This poem is incredible."

"Glad you think so. Nerval is one of my favorites."

We reach the teachers' lounge, our too-hot coffee cups burning our fingers. Madame Louis's voice rises from the big table next to the half-open window.

". . .yes, but it's better to preheat the oven to 180° C, and for the ingredients you need 250 grams of powdered sugar, 700 grams of flour, four eggs . . . oh, hi, Joséphine! Martin! Want a coconut snowball cookie?"

"Celebrating the next vacation already, are we?" Martin plays the sarcasm card.

"Oh, you're too funny. It's my birthday . . . I always make snowballs for my birthday. Don't you remember? Last year . . ."

"And the year before that." Hurley, the English teacher, hands us each a plastic plate.

"I don't remember. Maybe I wasn't teaching that day."

I say hello to the French intern, and to the economics teacher, who barely acknowledges me, her mouth full. I try to smile at the earth and life sciences teacher, while Madame Louis drops into her chair. Wearily, she reaches for another snowball from the almost-empty bowl on the table. She smiles, chewing, and sighs, her eyes watering as if she's just exerted herself greatly, or perhaps let out a fart. It's as if some emotion is coursing through her soft, shapeless body, making it quiver. Madame Louis is a Jell-O salad on the verge of tears.

"Happy, eh?"

After aiming this rhetorical question at her, Stéphane, the young science teacher, explains to us:

"She had a class today."

"She had a *quiet* class today," clarifies Hurley.

"Oh, yes, I'm very happy. I had fifteen minutes of pure, religious silence. And when that happens . . . well, when that happens, you remember why you're here, with them. You just have to hang in there, believe me; you just have to hang in there."

"You're so right, Madame Louis, our mission is to save lives . . ."

Martin looks at me, and we move away from the rest of the little group but don't have any time to talk. The bell rings. I drain the dregs of my coffee and kiss Martin on the cheek. Sometimes I think our lips are getting closer without us noticing.

I'm almost late for my dance class. After staying behind to meet with a parent, I dash for the bus, the train, the metro, determined to get there on time, determined not to lose a single second. Friday evenings are the best thing in my life. I walk from the changing room to the studio with the exaggerated stride of a dancer, on my tiptoes, in my twelve-centimeter spike heels. They look pretty damn good, these shoes. They give you a pair of legs you almost can't believe are your own. They make your chest swell with pride, with courage. They work miracles, is what they do. I'm marching off to war in this getup, and I plan to win. The mirror and I are finally on friendly terms with one another. It isn't my best friend yet, or even my buddy, but we're beginning to have a relationship. The mirror tells me about myself, and it's starting to say good things. One day, it'll love me. We'll be happy together. I think the other girls in the class are experiencing the same thing. Before I could look at myself in the mirror, I used to look at them, all of them, from head to toe. I learned their bodies like you learn a poem. By heart.

Fanny has the heavy thighs and swollen ankles of pre-menopause. Her legs are like tree trunks. She was the one who said that to me: "I've got tree trunks instead of legs." For months she wore pantyhose under her stockings. Fanny is funny. "We aren't all born a size small with skinny legs," she says, "no sense making a big deal out of it." She smiles at the mirror when we dance, at the teacher when she's explaining something, at me often. Last week, Fanny came to class without her pantyhose on. She looked at herself clinically in the mirror and murmured (but we all heard it), "You are my body, the only one I've got. We're going to get along a lot better from now on."

Jessica is perfect. Twenty-two, tall and slim with a few well-placed curves. Gorgeous ass, a dancer's arms, high cheekbones in a rounded girlish face. She's small-breasted, wears padded bras and has trouble with the nipple-tassels. "These 32A's aren't going to get me very far in life," she sighs.

Aude is fortyish and has the face of a Raphael Madonna and a chubby, babyish, porcelain-skinned body. She moves weightlessly, like a cloud. Once, she said, during the silent pause between two pieces of music: "Sometimes I really want to kill my children." She just came right out and said that, with no warning. Just spit it right out. We all had that idiotic look on our faces, the one you get when you're pretending not to have heard something.

And then there's Lucille, her belly slack after a difficult pregnancy. Desperate to get her pre-baby body—and her libido—back, she never takes off her waist trainer.

It was seeing their flaws that gave me the courage to look at my own. Our bodies are our history. We have to listen to our calf muscles, shriekingly tensed atop our dizzyingly high heels, our skin transfigured in that instant of forgetfulness that sweeps over us all, intoxicating us: "Tomorrow is the start of a new life." We dance until we're breathless; it's like a race, a dance of women overtaken by their own bodies. And this stocking I'm peeling off? Lo and behold, it's me, and it's Fanny too, and Jessica, and Aude and Lucille.

Back at home, I put my stilettos on the nightstand and gaze at them while I sip a beer. The heel fascinates me, sharp as an exclamation point; an order and a promise at the same time. Drinking my beer from the bottle, watching those shoes like

you'd watch a film, I feel a little bit masculine, and very femi-
nine. *Alive*, plain and simple. It must be because of the endor-
phins. But the biological cause doesn't matter. After class, my
thoughts and actions slow down. I sink into a kind of languor
in which something inside me gets activated. I take off all my
clothes and lie down on the floor with my eyes closed. My
body is my home. I see myself with new eyes in class. Maybe
I'm not so bad after all.

It's nine o'clock. I pick up my phone. If there's no answer,
I won't leave a message. I roll the scrap of paper with Andrea's
number on it around my finger. Like a lock of hair.

The spitball ricochets off the yellow-green wall and hits me hard in the left eye. I drop into a chair, hands covering my face. To achieve that kind of velocity, someone must have used a ballpoint pen casing as a blowgun. The tightly packed mass of my thirty-three students stops laughing and fidgeting. The spitball must have been a step too far. Silence. They're squeezed together, sometimes three or four around a table, in a projection room designed for twenty students at most. I think Lény's taking advantage of the situation to feel Wallen up. The girl is giggling, not even pretending to be shy about it. There are four students sitting at my desk and others on the floor, backs to the radiator. I could feel the wave swelling behind me as I fiddled with the DVD player, the rising tide, the threat of their imminent delight.

"Whoever did that, speak up now," I say, my eyes still closed. "If nobody comes clean, the whole class gets penalized."

Silence.

"Hadrien, go call the monitor, please."

Today was the first time I'd asked for a different room; I wanted to give the students a change of pace today. And it wasn't easy to pull off, either. The guy in the scheduling office wasn't happy when I put in the request with only five days' notice; I had to make excuses and sweet-talk the hell out of him to get him to do it. Normally we're required to reserve TVs or video projectors and computer rooms a week or ten days in advance. The office is usually swamped; the line's always busy, and there isn't even any music that plays while you sit there on hold. You start to feel like you're going deaf in the ear you've got clamped to the phone, like no one will ever pick up. Once your reservation is confirmed, you have to fill out the yellow form available in the student affairs office, but that slot in the rack is almost always empty. Teachers always snap them up as soon as the senior education advisor puts more out. I had to write my request on a sheet of blank paper. I got reprimanded for it. But I did manage to make enough of an argument for the educational value of this semester's film for my application to considered "complete." So my class on freedom now included watching several scenes from *The Matrix*.

The blue pill or the red pill? That scene gives us the opportunity to explore the question of choice, which is directly related to the question of freedom. There is no choice without freedom. I'd done my lesson-planning, proud of offering them something I thought was stimulating. There won't be a next time, that's for sure. No more films. Just philosophy, without pictures, and whatever happens, happens.

I leave the class under the monitor's stern supervision, but not before giving them an assignment: "Write an essay at least one page long, on a standard sheet of paper, on the following topic: Why is a spitball a spitball?"

In the nurse's office, they apply ice and warm water compresses to my bruised eye. I cancel my classes for the rest of the day. Down an eye, I'm on vacation. I cry discreetly. My heart is broken, and my legs feel like they are. I want to swallow an entire bottle of Xanax, and another one of champagne. Heartache is a defect; it turns us into dissolute beings. I thank the nurse and make my way to the principal's office. With my eyepatch, I'm in a fighting mood. Informed by the student affairs office, he's expecting me, for a meeting I requested as a matter of urgency.

"You're aware of the incident that happened with my senior class today . . . I'd like to file a report. I think it's my duty not to just let this slide, because . . ."

"I see, yes, very unfortunate. The fact is, though, you see, nothing like this has ever happened before, that I know of . . ."

"Things like this happen all the time, sir. The fact that we hardly ever report them, that we make do with a couple of compresses and day off to rest, means they're not punishable offenses. But not disciplining them, not reporting it—it's giving them permission to escalate. Next time, someone's going to lose an eye or, who knows, an arm . . ."

"Forgive me, but I think you're exaggerating. We don't have any problems with our senior students, and I'm the one who'll have their parents on my back if you decide to file a complaint—and it doesn't look to me like we know who's responsible. How can we be sure the incident happened the way you're describing it? You need witnesses . . ."

"I have thirty-three witnesses, sir, and a monitor!"

"Thirty-three witnesses who will never testify, as you well know! You weren't authorized to teach in that room. You put your students in an unsafe situation, which is a serious infraction. I mean, I understand; don't get me wrong. But what can I do? Go home; take a day or two to rest. You'll feel better. You need to rethink this thing when your head's clearer. And . . . well, if I may say so, it's also possible that you need to change your attitude toward your students. I appreciate your work, but I've also heard how demanding you can be, how strict. We're not here to traumatize them; you know that. Indulge them a bit. Catch their interest with relatable activities. Philosophy's a difficult subject. You may just need to adapt your approach and simplify it. That's it—simplify. The whole idea is daunting!"

I bow out, just to avoid bursting into tears in front of him. All the things I wanted to say to him but didn't whirl around in my head: *Philosophy is not an "activity," sir. Overindulgence is a crime. You've doubled my class sizes two years in a row now. I'll be submitting a report on today's incident.* All of these words I couldn't manage to force past my dry lips. My own power-lessness leaves a bitter taste in my mouth. I even forgot to pick up the incriminating spitball. Maybe I imagined the whole thing; my eye must have injured itself. In truth, though, I don't recognize how lucky I am. I work in a place where privilege means not having scissors and chairs thrown at you in class. That's what passes for good fortune when you teach in Drancy, a Parisian *banlieue* that's not exactly posh.

Come with your hair and makeup already done. You won't have time to get ready here."

I answer in monosyllables, yes-no-yes, goodbye. Breathless, my heart in my throat, like those first few minutes of the school year in front of a bunch of smirking new students, until I get used to it again. I've bought a black dress, long and completely sheer. Fanny gave me the address of a boutique in Pigalle. *It's not expensive, and it'll transform you*, she said. I'm finding it hard to believe that the body reflected in the mirror is actually mine. Following the advice of the woman on the phone, I chose a dress that's easy to take off. It's like a blouse, but without buttons. Andrea has an English accent. She smiles when she talks. You can feel it.

It's for this evening—Saturday—at 6:30. I haven't told anyone. I'm not even sure what I would say, except that I've always dreamed of auditioning. Auditioning for anything. The word itself encompasses a whole world that I'd love to live in. Art, freedom, beauty, performance. I don't feel the same about the word "competition," that's for sure. The oral exams were a bloodbath, and I was like a sacrificial lamb, but it wasn't my throat that got slit. My uterus coughed up blood for ten days. They thought it was an internal hemorrhage.

I've been training in front of the mirror every day. "Training" means looking at myself without feeling that little stab of disappointment that sends me diving headfirst into the Nutella jar. I was tempted to cancel this appointment even just an hour ago—but here I am, in front of Andrea, who is blonde, very blonde. She greets me with a smile that makes me smile back and then vanishes through a door that opens into a room decorated in purple, a dreamy-eyed brunette thrusting her ass toward me from a framed photo on the padded wall. Andrea steps in front of me and opens another door. Chairs on wheels and low, chunky tables are arranged around a plexiglass stage with a pole in the middle.

"You can change in the dressing room, in the basement," Andrea points to a flight of steps behind me. "You'll come up from downstairs and dance onstage. Is there a particular piece of music you'd prefer?"

I have no idea. I pretend to be thinking of a title, a singer.

"I can dance to anything; I'll leave it up to you."

The dressing room mirror is framed with track lights that stare back at me, emphasizing my dark circles and my dazed expression. It's like in the movies, all those movies where you see performers putting on their makeup, or taking it off, in front of mirrors lined with lightbulbs, with or without congratulatory bouquets. I take my concealer out of my rather sparse makeup kit and apply a little more under my left eye, the one hit by the spitball. There are tweezers on the dressing table, foundation-soaked sponges, and tiny neon G-strings; I've never seen ones so small. There's a box of Band-Aids, a rhinestone bracelet, some locks of false dark hair, and a stiletto heel that's come off its shoe. Despite the silence and emptiness around me, the dressing room feels full of life. I put on my lipstick. Reflected above my head are rows of platform shoes for pole-dancing. I turn around. Black and red and transparent and multicolored heels crowd the blue racks like clusters of arrows sunk into the flesh of some martyr. The customers are the martyrs here, I think. The racks are labeled with names written on strips of masking tape: Crystal, Electra, Divine, Sharon, Sofia. Photos of nude women with *no money, no honey* scribbled on them. I slip my new dress on without looking at my reflection. I feel like maybe I'm going too far with this. I'd rather not think about my body right now, which I'm sure must look obscene. I deliberately ignore all the mirrors that rise up imperiously as I pass. The makeup mirror, the large one on the wall, the small round ones, the bathroom mirror. I don't need them to make me feel like I exist. On the stage of my own wildness I can be anyone. The person I am in my dreams, maybe. Not myself, though, that's for sure. But a woman who isn't sad. Who isn't ashamed.

I let the door slam shut behind me and walk down the hall, hardly breathing. My head is down, and I don't know where I'm going, but my feet look fantastic in my new heels. I cross the leopard-patterned carpet in dimness barely relieved by the beams of the stage lights. I lift my chin, and Andrea smiles, the kind of smile that gives you confidence. Music. Pole. Twirl. Hair loosened to fall over my swaying shoulders. Look, look at my breasts. Beautiful, don't you think?

The music ends. What was it? What did I just dance to? Silence. I slip my dress back on. I did it. It was just a few minutes, but it was something important. One of those moments in life you think about when you want to feel happy for no reason. Happiness with no cause. A perfect thing.

"You're very graceful. And your breasts are magnificent; congratulations. You could be very successful, and make some decent money while you're at it. It's a yes for me. You can start whenever you like. Would tonight be possible? I don't have a lot of girls for Saturday night, and there's always a big crowd."

Start? Me? Tonight? Did I come here to "start"? I did it to do it, so I could say to myself, "There, I did it!" To be a nude dancer onstage for three minutes, that's what I wanted.

"I'd like to start as soon as possible"—the words burst from my lips like a cry of joy—"but I'm afraid I can't tonight."

It's a lie. In reality, I'm scared.

"That's okay. You can just let me know your availability."

She explains the rules while she shows me around the club. I trail after her obediently.

"When a customer asks you for a private dance, you have to take him into a room. No one in the main club can see what goes on in the private rooms, but there are cameras. You're always being filmed and monitored from the manager's office. It helps us protect you, and it also keeps the girls calm."

"Keeps the girls calm?"

"We actually have more problems with the girls than with the customers. A lot of the time, the girls are the ones who go a bit too far, to get their customers excited, get more money out of them. For a lap dance at the table you keep your G-string on, and it lasts for one song, that's it. If the customer wants you to keep going, he has to buy another ticket. They pay for the dances with tickets. In the private rooms, when you're completely naked, both of your feet have to stay on the floor. Don't let yourself be touched. Your job is to sell the performance of your body. That's all we ask you to do. If the customer touches you, you stop."

"So they have to pay in advance?"

"Yes, bearing in mind that you're not required to say yes to every customer. It's your choice. Customers have to buy tickets from the cashier to pay for dances, and then they have to give you those tickets. The tickets are your pay; you give them to the manager at the end of the night. I'm usually the one who keeps track of the number of tickets. You can accept cash, but within reason. Tips are okay, too. What you wear is totally up to you. I'll introduce you to Poppy. She knows all there is to know about this industry. I'm going to have her stay with you on your first night, help you with your first dances with the customers. And I'd recommend that you wear platform shoes, like the other girls. Stilettos look very pretty, but you won't get through the night in them. Oh—I almost forgot: have you thought of a stage name yet?"

"A stage name? No . . . I haven't."

"Here. This is a list of pseudonyms that no one else in the club is using."

"Actually, wait, I don't need it. I've got it! I'll be Rose Lee, like Gypsy Rose Lee! She's the one they invented the word 'striptease' for, in the forties. She's a burlesque legend; have you heard of her?"

"No, but I see you don't lack ambition."

Rose Lee. Maybe that's who I'm seeing in the dressing room mirror now. I'm wearing a black dress like hers. I feel like I'm inhabiting a new skin, infinitely softer than the old one. What if I really did this? Just for one night, to see what it's like? I could be this other woman, just for a night. The lipstick suits me; you might almost say I look pretty. I take one last glance in the mirror, to make sure my mascara hasn't run, that Rose Lee is fucking hot, and that she's really me. A fine sheen of perspiration covers my décolletage, giving it an extra glow. The excitement of sensing myself to be in a body I've missed, I'm sure. I don't know what I'm feeling, exactly. It's the feeling you get when your heart pounds, but you don't know whether it's from fear or desire.

Who cares what anything means? Isn't it better to live knowing that nothing really counts, that God is dead, that love is just one more illusion on a long list of them?

These are the thoughts I woke up with, the draw, the pull toward nothingness. I put a double dose of sugar in my coffee. I'm freaking out, and that's really what tastes bitter. After the high of the audition came the crash, and now reality is rearing its ugly head. I know nothing, absolutely nothing, about the world of the night, or men, or women, or myself, or my stupid fantasy of dancing nude. What the fuck am I actually going to do in that posh club near the Champs-Élysées next Saturday? Andrea wrote my name on the dancers' schedule. Well, she wrote *Rose Lee W*. The *W* made me think of a pair of wings. Later I realized it stood for *work*.

I put on my cotton granny panties to go into school. They're comforting, like a pair of fuzzy slippers for my mind. Comfort's important when you want to feel equal to a challenge; clearly this cut of panties was invented by a realist. For me, though, realism only lasts a few hours. Even before the sun goes down, I fling myself headlong into triumphant idealism: lace G-string, high heels, stockings. Just for myself. A little bit of intoxication to give myself courage. But my mind never stops working, the whole time. Am I a realist, an idealist, or a nihilist? That's the problematic of the morning. Not granny panties—nihilism. The students find the concept of

Nothingness fascinating. To them, thinking is a wasted effort. All those young minds dozing next to the radiator or doodling filthy pictures in class are running away; they prefer places where thinking is for losers. They smoke, they drink, they close their eyes and feel alive when the music hammers at their temples. Their indifference reeks of pot and beer. Teenagers have a pretty clear understanding of Nothingness. Maybe that's why I need to wear my granny panties when I teach: no pointless giddiness in the face of those empty minds.

In the hall on the way to the teachers' lounge, I'm surprised to see Hadrien leaning against the wall like he's waiting for someone. He shouldn't be here.

"Hi, Madame. Have you corrected the essays yet?"

"Not all of them . . ."

"I know who shot the spitball. He didn't mean to hurt you, but . . ."

"The matter is closed. I've informed the principal, and he'll be taking the necessary measures. Thank you, Hadrien."

I avoid his gaze, embarrassed by the loyalty of his gesture and the cowardice of mine. I never followed up, discouraged by the mountain of paperwork, the time I'd have to spend filling out forms that would do nothing but humiliate me that little bit more. I'm just like everyone else, that's what hurts, more than a spitball in the eye.

The pile of essays is sitting, unmarked, in my pigeonhole in the teachers' lounge. I pull Hadrien's paper from the stack, hating myself for lying to him twice. But the thought of slogging through a bunch of trite, witless writing, combined with the little thrill left over after the audition, has extinguished the spark of my good intentions.

"Jo? How are you?" Hurley has just come into the teachers' lounge.

"Hi. I'm reading essays . . ."

"You all right?"

"Oh yes, fine."

"You sure? Maybe it's just me, but I never see anything around here but the universal depression of the teachers . . ."

"That inevitable universality . . ."

"No point in thinking, Jo. When I'm upset I don't sleep, and then you know what I do? I dance in the dark. After a whiskey or two, that is."

He leaves as quickly as he arrived, without saying anything else, not even goodbye. "Dance in the dark." I understand better now. Hurley always seems to be running late, to be missing something. You can even see it in his clothes: loose trousers with no belt, shoelaces untied, shabby sweater. His socks definitely don't match. Seems like it's not just the students who believe thinking is pointless. I wonder what I'm doing here. I slide Hadrien's essay back into my pigeonhole. Another few weeks, and it'll be crammed with documents and memos and late homework. My great pleasure at the end of the school year is to throw everything in the garbage, even a few essays I never handed back. I slip a poem by Paul Valéry into Martin's pigeonhole. I copied it out for him on a sheet of aged paper, with my quill pen. He doesn't have any classes today; he'll find it tomorrow morning. It'll be a surprise. I cling hard to these little things that give everyday life some flavor. Like the square of chocolate I allow to melt in my mouth, to buck up my courage for the five hours of teaching that lie ahead, the two-hour gap, the papers to correct, the photocopies to make.

I can't wait to get home and take off these ridiculous panties.

M ost little girls dream of white dresses and contented marriages, or of being pop stars or businesswomen. Me, I dreamed of having a beautiful pair of breasts. I wanted breasts like the ones I'd glimpsed on the topless dancers on TV, one New Year's Eve, before my mother changed the channel. I thought about them every day. And every night before I went to bed, I repeated the same prayer:

"Please, God, give me breasts like the dancers in the rhinestones and flesh-colored fishnets. It's all I'm asking you for. If you can't do that, I'd rather be a tree instead. Amen."

At recess, the kids played kiss chase, but always without me. I sat with my back against the chestnut tree at the far end of the playground, away from their taunts, from the feeling that I wasn't one of them.

"Are you a girl or a boy?"

I asked myself the same question. I wanted to be like them, like the other girls, the ones whose little squeals I could hear as they let themselves be pushed up against the big hedge near the chestnut tree. The boy clutching the girl's waist and pulling up her skirt, eager-eyed, his hand groping at the childish white panties. She'd always have stopped pretending to resist by then. I would have let him do it, too, but I didn't wear panties. I always took them off when I went to the bathroom in the morning, before class. I'd stuff them deep into my book bag, just another white thing among the sheets of paper.

No boy ever lifted my skirt on the playground. Until I

finally filled out at twenty-two, my body had no dominant characteristics. Short hair, pudgy fingers, the sad-eyed gaze of a child soldier. One day I'd be a boy, the next a girl. I put on ambiguity every morning with the pink-and-blue of my over-sized track suits. Once I hit age twenty, I lost all hope. Just figured fate had passed me by, and gave up.

But sometimes, flowers bloom out of season. And nice tits, too. In spite of their belated appearance, my 36Cs provided irrefutable proof that I was a girl.

Now I feel sorry for flat-chested girls with their sad little sunny-side-up eggs nobody could ever make a feast out of, and mothers with their deflated bags in padded bras, and the nerds in their little-girl cotton undies. "It doesn't matter," they say, "because men fall for your brain, not your body." And I feel sorry for women who've had boob jobs, because, let me tell you, it doesn't get any better than a nice pair of natural breasts, and they don't cost a penny. I feel sorry for you, and I feel sorry for myself. Because I know the chaotic but overriding voice of a body that's being let go. The voice you drown out with the effort to lead a conventionally successful life, or with that four o'clock piece of cake, or dreams of pregnancy because children-are-pure-joy, or the eternal mantra *our bodies aren't the only thing that counts.*

But really, our bodies are the only thing that counts. Our bodies are all we have, and if we let them, they'll determine the course of our lives. Mine began the exact second I felt like I'd never seen anything more beautiful than the taut skin of my breasts, the rose-pink of my nipples pressing against my palms.

Did it really take me thirty years to be born? Yes, maybe. I dreamed of being the kind of sexy woman who gets men hard, drives them crazy, the kind who's not ashamed to show her ass and spread her legs. Turns out it's never too late to strip yourself bare. And at the end of the day, thirty-five really isn't old at all.

Back at home, I look at myself in the mirror. After thirty-five years, four months, and sixteen days, Rose Lee has been born at last. Her hair tumbling in dark waves over her shoulders, her skin tanned and perfumed, she stands naked in front of me. Her eyes gleam.

Rose Lee is me.

Saturday night, 10:15. I've been frozen on the corner for half an hour now, pressed up against the front of a closed boutique. Two hulking bouncers flank the front entrance of Dreams, their stony, silent faces blinking on and off in the light of its neon sign. I count to three, take a deep breath, filling my lungs like a free-diver. Time to take the plunge. I clutch the bag with my dress and shoes from the audition against my chest. I find myself unable to speak to the bouncers. The bulkier of the two opens the door and glances at the girl selling tickets in the lobby. She stops applying lipstick for a minute and looks up at me, throwing me a mechanical smile.

I step inside. I remember the décor, the purple walls, darker now in the dim light. The music thumps. In the main room, warm spotlights lazily caress the illuminated platforms. A dancer untangles herself from her lascivious pose around the pole to go up to a customer holding out a bill. She thrusts her ass toward him, and he tucks the money into her G-string. It's just like an American movie.

I head for the basement. The steps seem to shrink under my feet. My knees are jelly.

In the dressing room, half-open bags are piled on the floor, stage costumes spilling out of wide-open lockers, lingerie draped over chairs and G-strings scattered on the carpet. Ruby-nailed fingers adjust fishnet stockings and buckle high heels. Blond and dark and red hair gleams in the mirror, in curls or pinned into twists. A straightening iron smooths a recalcitrant extension. Dancers look appraisingly in the mirror; one girl gazes with satisfaction at the curve of her waist, while another scrutinizes the folds of her belly. I am in the antechamber of the femme fatale. It's like a La Redoute catalogue: breasts for everyone, from the very large to the very fake to the almost nonexistent. Perky asses and fleshy ones, smooth curves and the beginnings of cellulite; false eyelashes, eyelashes in plastic packets, perfectly symmetrical strokes of eyeliner. Asses and eyes, the same expression, the same honesty. Billows of pale flesh and UV-tanned flesh and black flesh, all equally, carelessly nude. All these bodies making a single female form, a single gaping pussy, obscene, hideously sexy.

I feel very small in my flat shoes, invisible in my loose clothing. I don't know what to do, or where to go. A blonde jostles me, her breasts bumping my forehead. There's no room for me in here, no empty chairs, not even a free spot on the floor for my bag. No one speaks to me. A few gazes land distractedly on me for a moment, like they know why I'm here but don't give a damn. The raunchy talk is louder than the roar of the hair dryers.

"I fucked him like crazy for five hours this morning. It was *insane!*"

I paste a smile on my face in a hopeless attempt to hide my embarrassment.

Where is Andrea? Which one is Poppy?

I turn. I'm humiliated now, on top of my fear. I make a beeline for the exit, switching on the scorn machine—*I've got nice tits, yes, but I also have a master's degree!* Scorn is great when you want to make it out with dignity. I'm just closing the dressing room door behind me when Andrea emerges from the manager's office, her ever-present smile firmly in place.

"There you are! Come on, follow me. Poppy is anxious to meet you."

In the chaos of the dressing room, Andrea points out a

brunette dancer curled up on a chair near the microwave, eating soup. Mouth outlined with deep red lipliner, sharp slashes of coral-pink blush on her cheeks, dark violet shadows of fatigue on her young skin. That's Poppy?

The girl dabs her lips with a napkin.

"You okay?"

"Hm . . .? Well, I'm pregnant, actually. But it's no big deal. I'm going to get an abortion. My boyfriend's not happy about it, anyway. I don't want to deal with the hassle."

Poppy gets up abruptly, tosses the cup of soup and the napkin in the garbage, readjusts her breasts in her push-up corset. Then she applies dark shadow to her eyelids and more red to her lips, blends the blush on her cheeks, rubs glittery lotion into her legs, puts on a delicate ankle bracelet. She's beautiful after all that. Like a pretty doll for grown-up children. I step a bit closer to her and look at her in the mirror. Poppy's skin has the sweet smell of a baby's.

"How old are you?"

She turns and looks at me with her beautiful eyes, not a crow's foot to be seen.

"I'm almost nineteen; my birthday's in a week and a half. How old are you?"

"Um . . ."

"No one cares about your age, just your outfit! Show me! And we'd better get you made up, or they'll have a fit. Have they given you a locker? You'll need to buy a padlock. Have you danced before?"

She seizes my bag, dumps it out.

"Is this all you have?"

"Er . . . yes, I'm on a trial period. I don't know if I'm really hired."

"A trial period? That's ridiculous, don't you think? Of course you're hired! Your dress isn't bad. And we share clothes a lot. This chick named Caro comes by selling them sometimes, too. Your G-string looks like a pair of briefs! Here, put this one on instead. It's ten euros. If you look next to the bulletin board, the clothes hanging there are for sale . . ."

Poppy hands me a pretty black G-string with rhinestones. It's miniscule. It freaks me out. How much of a woman's crotch can it possibly hide? My eyes dart around the room. Underneath the transparent clothes are nothing but strings and microscopic triangles of fabric that suggest hair-free pussies, ready to be shown off.

"You're not required to show your vag or your ass on stage. Just your tits. Let me see. Are they real ones?"

Poppy's like a greedy little girl. She cups my breasts with impatient hands. It's the first time a woman has ever touched me intimately like that. She weighs them delicately in her hands, running her palms along the curves and brushing the nipples with her thumbs. It makes me laugh. I don't know if it bothers me or if I love it. Some pleasures require indifference.

I slip my dress on. I don't regret buying it; Poppy seems to like it. She has me sit down in front of the mirror. I can't stop staring at my decolletage. The pink of my nipples plays hide-and-seek with the sheer black fabric. And here I thought I was dressed. I close my eyes, and Poppy dusts my lids with black shadow, and then brown, in copious layers. She describes the colors, the makeup techniques. She doesn't stop talking. With practiced movements, she applies eyeliner. I can feel the moist little tongue of the applicator near my bare eyelashes.

"Look up. Don't move!"

Poppy isn't done yet. I don't ask, *What are you doing? Aren't you finished? Is this Carnival, or what?* Being made up like this is the dream of the young girl I am now, here, beneath the grip of the tweezers and the eyeshadow, fascinated by the reds and browns, the ochre and orange and blue. With her painter's palette, Poppy is drawing me a new face. I'm going to have a body to make men rock-hard, to break their hearts. That's what being a woman is, too. Makeup and artifice.

I stare at the unmoving face in the mirror. It's like Rose Lee, but better. The eyes are enormous, darkened by eyeliner and mascara. The mouth is perfect. The cheekbones are high and rosy, like after a flush of emotion. Poppy rests her chin on my shoulder and contemplates her work.

"Soon you'll be able to do this all by yourself."

"You think so? It's not something that just happens spontaneously. You're all really beautifully made up. It's intimidating. You're all like . . . bombshells, ready to explode!"

"Never say to yourself, 'I'm not pretty.' It's not about being pretty. Doesn't have a fucking thing to do with 'pretty.' It's about being, like, totally desirable. You'll learn."

"Is that something you can learn?"

"Of course it is!"

"Being naked's not enough?"

"No, sweetie. *Strip* without *tease* is nothing but cat piss. Pointless!"

"So how do you do it?"

"Start by training yourself to look the customer right in the eyes. It's not easy at first because you're not used to it, because people don't do that in real life. You have to really stare at him, and when you get close to him, give him a little smile, like you're surprised, you recognize him, it's him, you were looking for him and you found him. The love of your life is right there in front of you. Then you get shy, maybe turn away a bit, look confused—a little modesty is reassuring to them—but then you start again, with a wink, for example, and get just a couple of centimeters from his face. After that, don't let him go! When you're in a private room and you're turned away from him, show him your profile, search for him with your eyes. Like that. Tilt your head slightly and look at him sideways— that's a killer! He won't know whether to stare at your ass or your face! Now you've got him! If he looks down when you stare at him, he's a goner! You're the woman he can't touch. Your neck, your thigh, your arm—they're the most beautiful things in the world. And don't forget that little smile. That makes them think you're getting comfortable now, and it's thanks to them. You're going to remind them of the main reason for their existence: getting a hard-on. That is *all* men live for."

"Men live for erections. Got it."

"Come on, girlie, with those big tits, you've got nothing to worry about! You're going to crush it. We'd better get up there now. Leave your bag next to mine. It'll be fine."

I feel vulnerable in the sheer dress and the G-string between my ass-cheeks. The heels, on the other hand, give me a little boost of confidence. I like being tall. I glance in the mirror one more time. Am I wearing just a bit too much makeup? All I can do for now is stick close to my mentor. I don't know what to do without this girl who knows everything and is taking me in hand. We go upstairs.

Poppy props her elbows on the bar and motions to the barmaid.

"Watch it," the girl says. "You start drinking too early and you'll be licking the customer's flies by two in the morning."

"Oh, fuck off! You gonna give me those two shots of vodka or not? Let me introduce the new girl, Rose Lee. She's got stage fright. Needs a little encouragement."

The barmaid, Ariane, winks at me and says, "You're in good hands," and then serves us two shot glasses filled to the brim.

"I'm not crazy about vodka . . ."

"Doesn't matter, sweetie. It's not vodka; it's fuel. You're gonna have to change your habits a little."

I'm in good hands. I imitate everything Poppy does: clink the glass, smile, deep breath, toss it back. The liquid scorches my throat and rises up somewhere in my brain. I turn, feeling a bit braver now, to have a good look at the room, this theater of the striptease artist. Bits of light rain down on the stages like confetti from mirror balls. Blue and red beams project upward from the platforms, shining on the girls arching their backs in perfect waves.

Poppy comes to stand beside me. "See her?" She points at a dark corner, away from the stage lights. "See that chick over there? She's new. Look what she's doing. She's gonna get chewed out by the boss. Never do that! In private, okay, but not for a table dance. She's letting herself go a little too far. I give her a month before she's a straight-up hooker."

A busty girl is rubbing herself urgently against a customer. Like a cat in heat, without instinct or desire. A skank. I feel sick. I turn my head and look at the stage again. I know I'm not dreaming, but nothing seems quite real, either. It's like the reality in here exists on top of the reality outside, making everything here into a sort of show. There are women here who can seduce a man just with the way they walk, with that tiny something extra that glints in their eyes. But some of the other dancers are clearly obsessed with their own reflection in the mirror; they're gyrating just to please themselves, *Mirror, mirror, on the wall.* Yet others are absolutely demanding the men's attention, going so far as to get down on their knees in front of them. Those are the ones crawling on their hands and knees, thrusting out their asses, offering them for a good hard spanking, arching their backs until they're practically bent in half, like glittering earthworms, shiny and polished as a convertible leading a parade, turning onto their backs and spreading their thighs wide, giving everyone a panoramic view—no charge for that—and the possibility of getting a glimpse into their shadowy depths. The men are consumed, lost. They see everything I don't, emanating from these bodies, to be bought with a few dozen euros.

This waking dream of mine is starting to look like a trashy TV show. Poppy seems to read it in my eyes, to notice the dulling of their sparkle.

"They're not all like that. Those girls make a ton of money; that's why they're here."

"I get it. The law of supply and demand."

"Yeah, but we're classy girls! There are plenty of customers for that, too! See over there? The glass of champagne?"

Poppy jerks her head subtly at a man down at the other end of the bar, leaning his elbows on the polished surface.

"He keeps looking over at you."

"Me?"

She motions to him. He smiles, drains his glass, heads toward us.

"Here she is, just for you. I'll leave you two lovebirds alone."

I'm here just for him. It makes me smile. He must be around forty, suit and tie, manicured hands. Probably just come from some office building in La Défense, or maybe avoiding a business dinner.

"What's your name?"

"I always forget who I am, when I come here. But what's yours?"

"I'm Rose. Rose Lee."

"Are you new? I haven't seen you before. Is that your real name?"

I don't answer.

We go downstairs, to one of the private rooms. He sits down, legs wide apart. I dart a furtive glance at the clock. He's paid for a three-minute dance. I can get through this. I slip my dress off. The rhinestone garter sparkles on my thigh, and the shadows are my makeup. He's only going to see what should get him horny. I hesitate for an instant. Where do I start? Poppy told me to arch my back, to throw my head back so my hair would tumble down almost to my ass. "Make love with yourself," she said. Knees slightly bent, I get my ass close to the customer. My G-string catches on his zipper. I cringe inside. I sit down quickly to hide the mistake. I lean back to rest my head on his shoulder and keep gyrating my pelvis, sliding a hand down to detach my thong. He must think I'm desperate to touch him, with my fingers fiddling at his crotch out of sight of the surveillance cameras. I stand up and face him. He's smiling. But why? I don't know if I'm being sensual or ridiculous, but it's not the end of the world. Finally, I sway my hips. Just enough time left to take off the G-string. I'm totally naked in front of a stranger who doesn't look at my waxed pussy even once.

It's over.

It must have taken three minutes, the minimum for a private dance. A hundred and eighty seconds, and bam. Thank you, goodbye. I'm a professional who respects the rules down to the second. Fear, it turns out, is just as effective as ethics.

"Get dressed and call the ticket-seller. Tell her to come down here."

"Why?"

"What do you mean, why? That was too short. I want more."

He buys half an hour. Then another half an hour. And then another whole hour.

He doesn't speak at all at first, his eyes straining in the dim light like a hunting dog's. He's very still, his arms spread out on either side of the bench seat like a torture victim. I sway closer and closer to his thighs, his crotch, his torso, his mouth. I straddle him—I saw some other girls doing it—and bring my cheek close to his; it's all I can do not to whisper *thank you* in his ear. Then he starts to talk:

"Sit down next to me. Don't put your G-string back on. I want to close my eyes and just smell your perfume, your skin against mine. Just stay there, naked, and don't move."

His hand is fiery-hot when he puts it on my knee and opens his eyes. I dance again, on his whispered order, which is more like a prayer. Me: movement, swaying, music. Time seems to telescope in on itself; we're outside time. But I have to keep track of it, this time is money, because, right now, that's what my body is. My hot tits are money. And his body is money, too, his body that reeks of whatever is making him unhappy, a sour smell, and the smoldering embers of his arousal. How can he be satisfied with just looking; how can he want to pay money to look? I'm offering myself up to a stranger because he's paid for it. I'm sharing my fee-for-service secret life with him, my makeup-masked, trembling fragility. We drink champagne. He's ordered a bottle of Ruinart. Poppy's right; it's fuel. We sit for a long time just holding hands, like two schoolchildren who can't find the words. I wonder if he loves me. I think I might love him as I rest my hand greedily on the thick wad of tickets in my garter, my money. He's just come from a poker tournament; he plays professionally. I feel like I'm on a movie set, filming a scene. Or in a dream. Either way, there's not a shred of reality in this private room where I'm selling the spectacle of my naked body. I want to dance, to make the perfect, voluptuous gestures I learned in striptease school, so his desire will come to nest in the palms of my hands, in the softness of my open thighs.

We go back upstairs together, still hand in hand, without speaking, each of us with our secret. He's waiting for me to dance onstage. I don't want to tell him it's my first time.

Rose Lee, stand by. Rose Lee, next! The DJ's voice resonates through the club. From the stage, spin after spin, bursting with excitement, knees like jelly, I cling to my customer's gaze. It's easier to exist in his eyes. But any time I look in the mirror, there you are, body, bathed in pink and blue lights, arched and unmoving: me, enthralled, not recognizing myself. Dark, piercing eyes, rosy cheeks, breathless, breasts on display like trophies. You, in the mirror, with your dilated pupils, scare me, tell me that just now in the private room that was really me gyrating near a stranger, me who felt like I might be dying because there was no anxiety, no shame in that dance I'd never danced before, only happiness—yes, happiness. I turn back to the audience. My customer's chair is empty. He's not there to give me his gaze anymore. I have to keep going alone.

The rush of adrenaline and a terrible kind of joy have kept me from sleeping all day. It's the alcohol, too, and the unending music, and the customer's desire, which took on the thickness of the stack of tickets, and the thought of my little bank account, suddenly flush. All of it. I just lie in bed, immobile, as if I'm paralyzed. Poppy's voice and the customer's interweave with my disordered thoughts, haloed by the intoxication that refuses to fade: "You lucked out, got a good one; there are a lot of assholes, too . . . cheapskates . . . phonies . . . lost souls . . . idiots . . . sometimes the best customers are the ones who've just been dumped by their girlfriends . . . *turn around, I want to see your back . . . say sweet things to me* . . . you screw whoever you want . . . but the customer has to be totally convinced that you can't see him outside the club . . . *sorry, I'm so hard . . . I can't bring myself to leave; can we go a bit longer?* . . . it's a self-contained world . . . pay special attention to the black credit cards . . . *you must be so disgusted with men; we're all the same . . . I don't even know your real first name* . . . make them line up for you . . . I'll tell you which ones are lowlifes, but it's none of our business . . . *I want to lick you all over* . . . you have to recognize the prostitutes that come in with the customers; they'll do what we won't, they're there to finish them off . . ."

My first customer's name is David. I'll never see him again. He's moving to Stockholm tomorrow, to be closer to his two-year-old daughter. I stayed naked for hours to please this stranger, and it felt perfectly normal.

There's no racket, no yelling or shoving in the hall on the way to the classroom. That's normal. It's Monday; everyone's still asleep. I have to weave my way through a chaotic mass of backpacks to reach the door. Nobody moves aside; there isn't even the faintest instinct for ordinary politeness. Just a jumble of black and pink and blue tracksuits slumping against the wall. Inanimate bodies, closed eyes above silent mouths. I prefer them this way, sleepy and absent. Especially today. My legs are still shaky from the otherworldly night I spent as Rose Lee. Sunday, on no sleep, I worked like crazy. Thirty essays corrected in one sitting, just so I'd have something else to focus on, so I wouldn't think about it anymore. Was it so bad, that sensual hand, ashamed of being so eager, that caressing hand, stretching out for the tickets and toward the customer's face? A lot of the essays I marked weren't worth any more than three or four points out of twenty, and I didn't even correct the misspellings: *happyness, phylosophy, Buddist enlightenment, efemera, simpilstic approach*. I read thoroughly, without ever feeling like I wanted to die, or mocking the poor student everyone looks at with pity, powerless to help. Suddenly infused with soaring pedagogical passion, I gobbled down those thirty unpalatable essays, which strayed off-topic almost more often than not, as if I were taking a peaceful stroll on a summer night at nine o'clock, gazing at a beautiful sunset. I kept repeating to myself that my place is here, among these underprivileged students, and not in one of those other Parisian schools I request to be transferred to every single year. And *definitely* not in a nightclub, showing my ass to anyone willing to fork out the cash for it. Compassion flooded through me, along with a tear or two, sanctifying my exalted state of mind. Thank you, students. Thank you, Hadrien. I knew now why he'd waited for me, all alone, by the teachers' lounge. It wasn't just about the spitball. He'd wanted to know if I'd read his letter. I'd found an envelope taped to the last page of his essay, on which he'd written simply, "For you."

Drancy, November 15, 2005

Dear Madame Professor,

I don't really know where to start.

I'm sorry I've said philosophy was pointless, more than once. I really, really didn't mean it. I know I'd hate it if someone told me football was pointless. I swear I'll never say it again.

Ever since middle school, my mom's been saying, "You'll see when you get to your last year, philosophy will make you understand life, you'll see, you'll see." And now it's my last year, and I don't feel like philosophy is helping me understand life. I like it, sometimes, though. I repeat phrases in my head from the texts you have us read.

Speaking of that, I wanted to ask you a question, but not in front of the whole class. So I'm writing you this letter.

I twisted my ankle over the weekend and didn't go to football practice. I spent the whole weekend in bed, staring at the ceiling and waiting for the swelling to go down. It's weird; I kept imagining things while I was looking at the cracks in the ceiling. I don't know if it's normal, because it was like when you're a little kid, staring at the clouds and thinking up stories. It was like ten thousand things came into my mind, and I remembered that once you said, "Take care of your inner

*life." I remember I didn't say anything when you said that,
and then Amine came out with something like, inner life
wasn't life, it wasn't even reality, it wasn't anything. But
while I was lying in bed like that, all these thoughts just came
to me, all by themselves. Is that what inner life is? If that's it,
I'm wondering if it's always negative. Because I thought to
myself that life is a crack, like in the ceiling. Maybe it's stupid. I guess I'm not the only person who feels like I'm nothing. I admire you when you talk about how important intel-
ligence is, and you say we need to fine-tune our abilities. But
to do what, Madame? If life isn't all happy stuff and it beats
you down? Life is like me, last weekend; it needs crutches.
Don't you think life beats you down, Madame?*

*Anyway, I don't know if I'm making any sense. I just
wanted to tell you that, right now, I don't feel like philosophy
helps you live your life better. You said that, too, I remember
it clearly: "Philosophy helps you live your life better."*

Thank you for thinking about my questions.

Yours truly,

Hadrien

I rummage in my bag, my mind a tangle of confused, guilty
thoughts. I know Hadrien is here, but I don't look up at him. I
search. No key. I mutter some vague excuses—"Just don't go
anywhere."—and run back toward the teachers' lounge, going
fast enough to lose my breath, fast enough to risk falling. We—
teachers—we can't leave them unattended. We can't take our
eyes off them, ever. The last time that happened was during
Madame Louis's math class. Five minutes left unsupervised was
enough for one girl to claim she'd been groped, for a window
to be broken, and for a backpack to disappear with all its contents. You can't let them go to the bathroom, you can't ever give
them permission to leave the classroom, and you can't ever have
any physical contact with them. The students are untouchable.

No hand on their shoulder to encourage them, or to hold them back. No touching, ever. Superintendent's orders.

Returning with the key, I realize just how total their lethargy is. No one has moved a muscle, paralyzed by exhaustion, or maybe boredom. I open the door. They drag their carcasses, weighed down by backpacks, to their seats. Some of them thud noisily down into their chairs, others are already rocking back and forth in seats that sound like they're about to crack, staring vacantly into the distance. I keep my mouth shut, thinking of the instructions we've been given: don't ask students to sit up straight; it disturbs their concentration. Superintendent's orders. From my desk at the front of the room, I watch them fidget, catching glimpses beneath their restless movements of the violence that is always there, ready to explode, shoving a classmate, scraping their chair legs on the floor, once, twice, for no reason except to be a pain in the ass: the low rasping sound of the chair legs is like some kind of sinister music. I stand in front of them silently, my heart lurching with every rasp. I watch them drum and pull and fiddle and toss, and it's my flesh they're abusing. It paralyzes me. The few that aren't sprawled almost horizontally in their chairs, heads low, stare at me with disapproval. I take a swallow of water to get my voice back. Hadrien is silent. He's sitting straight-backed in his chair. I meet his eyes, finally, and the words I need to say, the right words, suddenly come out:

"I don't like getting up at six o'clock either . . . but there are things to do that are more important than sleeping. This morning, we're going to do an essay model for the problematic you had for your homework: "Can a person be happy without being free?"

I write the phrase on the board as a babble of protest rises up behind me.

"What about our papers, Madame?"

"After the essay model."

"But that won't help us; we won't ever be able to write it like that; we just want our grades!" Little Wallen is whining, refusing to let it go. "Essay models are for rich kids' schools."

"Yeah, she's right," puts in Leïla. "And anyway, we have the right to get our papers back."

The standoff with the students is exhausting me. I've got a migraine coming on, I can feel it. I pretend not to hear them; I can be stubborn, too. I write out a possible problematic for a typical essay: *Are happiness and freedom incompatible? Part one: Freedom is an obstacle to happiness. Part two . . .*

Behind me, the muttering hasn't stopped. Stifled giggles. A chair falls over. Is that the sound of someone vomiting? I turn around. Leïla is on her feet, her cheeks bright with fuchsia blush, her pink tracksuit skintight, hair unkempt.

"Madame, Lény farted! I'm so sick of guys! Why can't we have girls-only classes?"

"Oh yeah, right, your words are farts! You're farting with your mouth! That's Diogenes, Teach! Like girls' farts don't stink . . ."

The class is in total disarray. The words burst out of me: "Zip it, Lény!"

"Why should I zip it, Madame? I didn't do nothing wrong. You're not supposed to hold farts in. They're made to come out; otherwise you get sick."

I don't reply. How can I argue with such wisdom?

So, happiness. And freedom. No notebooks on the tables, pens scattered everywhere. Whenever I'm given a few minutes, I try a little reflection, a little exploration. It's intermittent philosophy, a tiny seed here, a tiny seed there. You can't stop sowing the seeds and hoping for a harvest. It's the fundamental purpose of the job.

"Being happy requires learning to choose . . ."

"Choose what, Madame? Tomorrow's pill? That one's not red . . ."

"Happiness is the only goal we have that's just for ourselves."

"Yeah, but I also want my brothers and sisters to be happy!"

"You can't be happy without being free . . ."

"Cool, yeah, that is so fucking true!"

"What about you, Madame? Are you happy?"

Hadrien, who hasn't spoken until now, repeats the question:

"Madame? What about you? Are you happy?"

Stop pestering me, Hadrien. Stop asking me to care about you. I have nothing but philosophers to give you, concepts and quotes so well formulated that you'll feel like you understand the world, life, yourself. Listen to me, just listen to me and study; do what I ask you to do. This isn't for the bac. *Screw the* bac. *This is for you, a gift for life, a spark to guide you in the dark.* I blush. I want to run away. Or cry. Again. Always crying, that's what powerlessness is. At this precise moment in time, Hadrien, seventeen years old, and all his scruffy, youthful glory, are stronger than I am.

"Yes, Hadrien. I am. It makes me very happy when you understand the lesson, when you react like you've done today and we try to have a discussion. I'm happy to give you back the first essays of the year. I wanted to encourage you, even though we still have a lot of work to do."

Nothing but idiotic words. I don't believe them myself. No one believes them; no one gives a damn. I look down at the stack of papers. I hand them to Wallen so she can distribute them. Hadrien leaps out of his chair like a sprinter at the sound of the gun, to help her pass them out. I've run out of words. It actually feels like I've lost my voice. They don't care what I say anyway, and at any rate, they're the ones calling the shots. A few minutes later, Hadrien hands me back an absent student's essay and murmurs, almost inaudibly: "I'm waiting for your answer." I look up, look him straight in the eye, without meaning to, like a reflex, an action too urgent, too necessary to try to fight. I like this boy. I've taped my letter to the last page of his essay, just like he did.

Paris, November 25, 2005

Dear Hadrien,

First of all, I want to thank you for the attention you're paying to philosophy, and to my classes. I don't think you're "against philosophy." On the contrary, I think you're very much "for philosophy"; you've already taken the first step toward what I would call a philosophical attitude, which is a reflective attitude. You might remember the definition of "reflection" we talked about in class: "an act of thought turning inward on itself to gain an understanding of its own workings." If it took twisting your ankle and spending the weekend in bed, staring at the ceiling without even listening to music, for you to reach this point, then I must admit I'm thankful for your temporary handicap. The images that those cracks and mildew inspired in your mind were none other than your thoughts. Your questions, and your letter, are wonderful examples of reflective consciousness. You are the subject, making your thoughts the very object of your thoughts. That dialogue of thought with itself—that is philosophy, my dear Hadrien. But I understand your doubts, and I want to try to answer your questions. You're wondering if philosophy can spare us the pain of existing, soothe our worries, and give meaning to everything in our lives that feels meaningless. I understand, and I share your anxiety. You don't need to be a philosopher to sense the absurdity of existence. Often it's the questioning itself that makes us anxious.

Yes, Hadrien, philosophy can help us to live our lives better, because it teaches us to work on our perception of the world and of ourselves, our desires and our anxieties.

Yes, Hadrien, it's true that philosophy itself doesn't bring happiness. While philosophizing can be a pleasurable thing, it's not because we philosophize that we are happy.

You've understood correctly that at the root of all philosophy is some original disappointment, an unhappiness. Stuck in bed with a bum ankle, you start thinking. It's when you can't stand up—Is it really life that can't stand up, or maybe you? Or all of us?—that you start to reflect. Strange, isn't it? Maybe the mind and the body are limping, but life, far less so.

Dear Hadrien, I want to tell you that life is exciting, irresistible, that you have to fling yourself headlong into it, savor it, love it every day, every minute, more and more deeply. But I owe it to myself to remind you that it's sad and repetitive, too, and not without its share of vulgarity and ugliness and mediocrity. And there's always the threat of illness, and the final defeat of death.

It was philosophy that taught me that there are ideas that can save us, and others that can ruin us. Knowing how to live means choosing the ideas that won't ruin us. That's how philosophy can rescue us from the unhappiness of existing.

Don't forget: Seneca said, in On the Shortness of Life, *"It takes the whole of life to learn how to live."*

Thank you, Hadrien, for sharing your ideas and your insights with me.

Sincerely,

Joséphine

PART TWO
THOU SHALT NOT TEMPT

I'm a fantasy.

For ten days I've worn nudity like a mask. I've called myself Rose Lee, and I feel like Rose Lee is me. My new figure, made svelte by depression, has been providential.

I look over the pile of homework on the table. Dead tired, I've never been so alive. I hardly sleep at all anymore; my nights now are full of daylight. I'm joyful in a way I didn't know it was possible to be. I can feel my body turning liquid, almost melting into the chair where my venerated ass feels again, shamelessly, the sensations of last night's gyrations. This is what it means to be a sexual fantasy: sinking into your own pleasure.

I gaze at the thirty-three students in front of me without seeing them. They have ceased to exist. I hide my awe-struck eyes with their dark circles behind a pair of glasses. I am totally dazzled, completely blown away. I've never felt beautiful. Not even pretty. Every woman deserves to feel this giddy, this dizzy with power. I had no idea how life-changing men's gaze on a woman's body could be. I didn't know, because I was scared. Scared of men, yes. Scared of their hard-ons and their uncontrollable libidos. How do I admit, now, that I want to be the woman who gives every man on the planet an erection? The handsome ones and the ugly ones, the old and the young, the good men and the assholes? The ones I desire, and the ones I don't?

At night, I am that woman. I am Rose Lee. I dance completely naked for anyone willing to pay for the show. I always touch myself a little, and a little more every time, to make sure I'm doing the job right. I watch the other girls a lot. I want to learn. It reminds me of the ballet classes I took when I was young; the sideways glances at each other's *battements* and *ports de bras*. The girls always used to stay naked in the dressing room, before and after the shower, sitting together, gossiping. I envied their serene nakedness, their natural femininity. They were beautiful without artifice, striking without provocation. Women exposed without being stripped bare, unassailable in their womanhood. I always tried to hide myself around them, concealing my body behind a bath towel. I got dressed fast, as fast as I could. But now I want to be like my colleagues; I want their knowledge, so I can be the queen of hard-ons.

Narcissistic satisfaction. Yes, and so what? It's about men admiring my tits now, rather than assessing my lesson plans, and goddamn, it feels good! Have I lost it completely, feeling more like a philosopher onstage than I do in front of my students? I wonder, but for me it's only onstage that my life is neither sad nor tragic. Living is easy there, and freedom is an emotion, not just an idea. Not to mention the money. That wasn't the reason I started doing this—I hadn't even thought about it. But when you earn your entire monthly teacher's salary in just a few nights of dancing, you suddenly forget all those books you've read and reread and summarized. Who said money can't buy happiness?

I know, now, what's expected of Rose Lee. Poppy explained it perfectly. Men want me to play the game. First, Rose Lee has to stare at the customer, to face him head-on, but from a distance at first, while he gets comfortable in his seat. Make him wait a minute or two. Search his eyes for that spark of desire. Then she has to come closer, soft and swaying. That's how it has to start, with a kind of dizziness, where he doesn't know what's happening to him, where he stares at his ideal woman like a deer caught in the headlights, stunned. He needs to want to feed from her open mouth, to suckle, to talk, all at once. But the only expression on his face will be one of impatience, as the minutes tick by without him getting what he wants, while Rose Lee's eyes flick callously to the time-counter on the wall of the private room. But she'll be able to make him feel like time is standing still. She'll make him hope for a kiss, her mouth hovering close to his, trailing a finger down the side of his dumbstruck face. And then she'll clutch him to herself, watch as he lets his head fall back on the bench and closes his eyes, to shut out the sight of her. He can't touch Rose Lee. He knows it. A lot of the time, he doesn't even dare. Or he will just graze her very carefully, very slowly, his hand brushing her wrist, or his fingers closing around the heel of her shoe. If he gets pushy, Rose Lee might pretend to strangle him—Poppy told her about that little trick—or grab a fistful of his hair, shaking her head gently. If he's too calm, she undoes the top button or two of his shirt and acts like she wants to caress his chest, to get him excited, so he'll ask to extend the dance.

Another man might be crude, watch her with lust in his eyes, say dirty words to her. He's like an animal in heat, rubbing his erection through his pants and ordering her to rub herself against him. Then she has to smile, but without doing anything he says, without betraying her contempt for him. When she's naked, he wants to see her pussy, he asks her to spread her legs: "I can pay more for it." He takes advantage of that second when she's moving away to try to touch her with his dirty fingers. She turns and slaps him. He stops twisting his hand inside his underpants and humiliating her with his words and ejaculates in his pants, quickly dropping his gaze, looking away.

When that happens, Rose Lee has to handle herself elegantly, smile, make light of what has just happened. It's written in her contract: "The artist acknowledges that she may be exposed to nudity and sexually explicit talk, and may witness explicit sexual actions and behavior, and declares that she does not find such situations offensive." Everything calms down and fades. She gets dressed silently, waiting impatiently for him to open his eyes and pay her for his indecencies. She keeps an eye on the hand rummaging in his pocket and holding out more tickets. And then she walks away from him, maybe forever.

He's a stranger.

The forgettable man.

He and all the others are a multitude and no one, all at once.

Rose Lee is a nude dancer. Her world is made up of two large rooms, three stages with three poles, and ten private rooms. Five hundred square meters of dimly lit happiness.

Be smart, not beautiful. Beautiful women aren't good for anything except as an extra jewel on a rich man's arm. Don't be seductive; be invisible. No makeup, no dresses, no high heels. Never spread your legs for a man. Men only know violence; all they care about is satisfying the animal inside them. Don't daydream. There are no princes, and no princesses.

I'm four years old, my hair in a crew cut, my room full of encyclopedias and children's literature, even though I can't read yet. But not a single doll. My mother has decided that my ugliness will be my salvation, that being cultured is the way to true happiness. Every month she buys a few new books for my library. I envy the bedrooms of my classmates, with their candy-pink walls and ceilings decorated with stars that glow when you turn out the lights. Clustered on shelves by their beds are boy and girl baby dolls, tiny pacifiers atop stacks of doll clothes, Barbies in stiletto heels with their miniature kitchens. I only had one doll during my childhood, a Barbie given to me by Delphine, a girl in my class. Its hair was totally destroyed, but I decided the wild strands gave my Barbie a fierce look. She was an adventurer, the heroine of all the outlandish stories I made up for her. I loved her that way and hid her in the doghouse that belonged to Mac, the philosophy-teaching neighbor's Great Dane.

One day, my Barbie disappeared. I looked for her everywhere.

Of all the girls, I like Fleur best. She's different from the others. Fleur dances with her rounded, perfect ass, with her hands, with the curls that brush her shoulders, with her eyes. Especially with her eyes. When she sways her hips, her eyes glow brighter than the stage lights. She looks out at the audience, rests her chin on her shoulder, and flutters her eyelashes like you do when you're just about to come. Fleur arouses desire with her whole body, arches her back, thrusts her ass at the audience, smiling at me—*That's for me*, I think to myself—and I find my gaze drifting down to the soft fold that separates the top of her thigh from the curve of her ass. I look at that thrilling little expanse of pink flesh, and I think of the person who will run a tongue along it, wondering if her pussy is as perfect.

There's shouting in the dressing room tonight. Late again, Fleur has gotten into a screaming match with Andrea. She's stubborn as a mule, they say, and one day it's going to get her fired. It's almost happened many times already. But it makes me want to get to know her better. I don't approach her, but I watch her: she caresses the back of the customer's neck, runs her fingers through his hair as if every stranger is the man she loves. Fleur touches before she speaks. She gets intimate without being invited. The men smile, confused, already speechless except for the word *yes* repeated over and over and over. That's what gets her whole nights in a private room. Fleur is a safe bet. And she brings a ton of money into the club, so they put up with her, for better or worse.

After the argument with Andrea, Fleur's smile onstage is a little bit ambiguous. The thick layers of mascara and the under-eye circles she doesn't conceal tonight make her gaze dark and troubled. Her smile doesn't reach her eyes. She drops to her hands and knees on the Plexiglas platform, stands up, the blue stage-lights striping her arched back and bathing her naked breasts, which she caresses absently, mechanically. She slaps her own ass with both hands. Fleur is the animal you want to whip. That's what gives her the advantage over the rest of us.

Stepping down from the stage, she drops a cigarette she had tucked away in her bra. Instinctively I bend to pick it up and hand it to her, wordlessly. She takes the cigarette and then laces her fingers through mine. "Come with me," she says. "I've got a guy warmed up; he's waiting for me. You can take care of his friend." I don't say yes or no. I have no real preference either way. I just let myself be towed along, like an object.

It's four in the morning. We've been in the private room for about two hours now, drinking magnums of Ruinart with our customers. Fleur's clitoris is pierced. I can see it gleaming in the semi-darkness. This is the first time I've ever seen her completely naked. I thrust my ass at my customer, my back to him, my eyes straining into the darkness for a glimpse of her pussy, her legs, her dancer's foot, perfectly pointed. I follow her movements as she edges closer to her man, who stretches his hand toward her breasts. It annoys me. I remind him of the rules: no touching. Fleur laughs. She grasps the man's hands and guides them closer to her body, toying with his desire, and maybe with mine, too. There's nothing but one tiny, insignificant centimeter separating the man's hands from her bare flesh. This girl is a vixen. I stop dancing and just stare at her. As soon as she lets his hands go, the customer seizes her and jerks her toward him. He sticks out his tongue, clearly desperate to suck her nipple, but stays sitting down, like a kid, focused on his ultimate desire, mouth gaping like a salivating dog, kept at a distance by the suddenly tensed length of Fleur's arms. One of his hands manages to grip her thigh, the other scrabbling for her smooth pussy. I can't take it anymore. There's no more music. It's just Fleur, and her body, prey for those ravening hands. In a matter of seconds, though, she exacts her revenge and reestablishes her supremacy. Lips curling in a disdainful smile, she grabs her half-full glass of champagne and dumps it on the client's crotch. "Sorry," she laughs. "That was an accident. But what the fuck are you playing at? You know it's against the rules to get off in here! You'll have to pay extra, or I'm calling the security guys." Fleur draws me toward her and whispers: "Don't worry, it's no big deal. He's just a man, look at him." She hugs me and smiles at the customer, who pulls out two hundred-euro notes. I follow her lead. We extend our naked thighs with their rhinestone garters: *here's the piggy bank, thank you, it'll be over before you can blink unless you buy some more tickets. We've had some fun tonight, haven't we, you naughty boys?* I cuddle up to my customer one more time, trailing my tongue along his neck. I'm not enjoying it—that's because of the tingling between my thighs and Fleur, who won't stop smiling, simulating desire with uncanny perfection. I gather my few things from the floor while she vanishes without a word. Another man is waiting for her impatiently at a table. Everything goes too fast. She doesn't so much as glance at me again until the end of the night, when she suggests that I come with her to the after-party at Queen with the DJ and an American friend of hers who's some kind of house music celebrity.

"I thought you'd stay with that guy."

"Which guy? The last customer? That numbskull from before?"

I feel like an idiot.

At Queen, everyone dances in the VIP area.

"You like Fleur, huh? You like girls?" The American asks questions without waiting for my answers.

I've never liked a girl.

The music makes everything blurry, and Fleur just keeps dancing, dancing, her arms flailing wildly; she's gorgeous, bathed in psychedelic lights. The DJ shouts in my ear: "The American likes you! He wants you to go to Chicago with him! You should go!" I don't say anything. I don't have anything to say. I'm not sure I understand what's happening. I don't know what I want, either. And anyway, the sudden hammer-blow of reality comes slamming down to spoil the party: I have to be at school in about six hours. Fleur comes close, suggests a foursome. I pretend I don't understand; I can't stay; I really have to leave.

"Come on, we'll both go," she says. "Let's go get a nice steak; that'll perk you back up." But I'm not hungry; I'm about to collapse with exhaustion. And steak isn't really something I tend to crave at seven o'clock in the morning.

Fleur stops trying to persuade me and walks me out, holding my hand like we're a mother and her little girl, her lips against my cheek. She scans the still-deserted street and hails a taxi. "Let's talk soon," she says, taking out her phone and waiting for me to give her my number. "I've got to take a few days off, but I'll be back next week. Are you working then? I'll have some customers requesting me, you'll see; we'll make good money together like tonight. Did you enjoy tonight?"

I don't have time to answer. Fleur slides her left arm around my waist and kisses me on the mouth. Her tongue finds mine.

A taxi pulls up, waiting.

Just before leaving the private room tonight, Fleur's customer dropped to his knees at her feet and licked her high heels. She hadn't given him access to her toes—"That would cost more than you have," she'd said, like a true vixen.

I'd love to be a vixen, too. Men don't scare me anymore—

not forgetting that, in places like my club where they choose who gets in the front door and who doesn't, the customers are obedient, like dogs walking on their hind legs, and aren't supposed to move a muscle unless you tell them to. They're an annoyance. They'd rather whine and grope discreetly at their bulging zippers and close their eyes so they can't see what they can't touch. There are a lot of submissive men out there. It's surprising. They pay to experience what they'd never put up with in the real world—a naked woman who makes them think she'll fuck them and ends up being a tease instead. It's a cruel game, but it has hidden virtues. In real life, desire isn't likely to be perfect—but in here, that's possible. That's what they're paying for. That's what they're buying. I watch them carefully. Their urges are absolute, their desire hyperbolic. In the many stories they tell about their private lives, the women often refuse to satisfy them, even making fun of their daily needs for love and eroticism. When a couple is solidly in a relationship, or after a pregnancy, the women—these men say—stop wearing makeup or taking care of their skin and hair and fingernails. They'd rather just be mommies; they become untouchable. On my knees in front of an erect cock I won't actually see, entwined with a man, letting myself be penetrated by his eyes, begging, passionate, almost tearful sometimes, I know I will never feel what they do. A kind of crazed ardor that women simply lack. I dance naked around that lack, that empty space.

If the music didn't stop, and the night didn't end, if we couldn't come out from behind the curtain, I'd go all the way. I'd give certain parts of my body, like gifts. Because Rose Lee has an entire harem of men at her disposal. She can help herself to them as she pleases. What would you do, women, with all these men on their knees before you, trembling and swooning? You, protected by anonymity and totally free? Have you ever thought about it? Have you wanted it? It scares you, doesn't it—the idea that you might like it? Putting on the mask of Rose Lee turns me into a free woman. I don't have to answer to anyone. I tell myself that over and over, to drown out the tiny, sly, shameful voice that sneaks in during those first moments after I wake up in the morning: am I a whore? For just a few moments, Rose Lee is the troubled memory of the night just spent nestled between the legs of strange men with stiff cocks and hungry, empty hands. Every morning is a chance to understand, to do the right thing. To end the charade, the night, to say to myself, *Okay, there, you're very brave, you did it, you've had your revenge, had the last laugh at all those little shits from the school yard, and every boyfriend who dumped you too fast, and the mirrors where you saw the ugliest girl in the whole world.* But that doesn't take into account my joy and pleasure, strong and intense as an electric shock. The customer, like a thousand other men, pressed against me while I'm totally nude, with the disarming tenderness of their helpless arousal, which shouldn't please me, but does. That's what banishes my shame behind the curtain of the private room, in the half-light where I'm intertwined with a man keeping his hands on the bench seat.

In his weary eyes, I'm beautiful.

4

The front door is broken, and I have to wait for the monitor to come let me in. I'm late. Still wrapped tightly in the night where Fleur was nothing but a dream, I didn't hear my alarm clock. So much for my first hour of teaching. Six months ago, I would have shown up at school with my face ravaged by guilt, repentant as if I'd committed some horrible sin, begging for forgiveness. No longer. After quickly calling the school, I took my time getting ready. When I first wake up, I need time to remember who I am, to formulate my to-do list amid the chaos of my thoughts: wear loose, drab clothing, definitely nothing designer, definitely nothing fashionable, hair in a knot, little or no makeup. I need to give the impression of having just gotten out of bed. Measured smile, neutral expression, dull-eyed, if possible. In short, I need to play the part of my job so no one will notice me. There can't be even a trace of Rose Lee in my accessories or the under-eye concealer that matches my complexion, not a hint of a sparkle in my eye. Every day I have to remind myself of this, because I feel like I'm disappearing beneath the power of the night. Jo is fading away because Rose Lee's world is becoming more and more familiar, its emotions dispelling the boredom and bitterness of my days. At night, we talk. I've never talked so much. At night, we smile. In the teachers' lounge, we hardly even say hello; we start the day with a grimace. And in the afternoon, as five o'clock approaches, we even stop looking at each other, too eager to get out of there, to run like cowards.

Exhausted. A few might manage a smile that doesn't reach their eyes. Do your job. Hang on. No question of laughing, not least because the pay, one more grudging concession from the law and order government, is right on par with the amount of recognition and thanks we get. It's a truly wretched existence, one that drove me to seek stimulation by reading the great philosophers. Where the hell did I get the ludicrous idea of finding happiness in thinking? I wrapped myself up in concepts to forget my own misery, and the misery of existence. I added my voice to the doleful chorus of intellectuals everywhere: *Life, what suffering!* But no more suffering now. Here I am, stripped naked, finally. I've stopped taking antidepressants. No more therapy sessions. Now I buy makeup, and more lingerie. I need Rose Lee, her perfume that envelops me like a magical charm, my new inner life that's like music I can dance to. The night is my brightest day, a perpetual present of brilliance and well-being. It's life without classes and meetings and the worries that crush my spirit, where the world and my fellow humans have a presence like nothing I've ever known. It's almost a kind of perfection, where there's no longer any need to ask the metaphysical question *Why?* The truest luxury—the truest happiness, maybe—is to exist without sorrow, without limits: to linger around a drink, a game, an encounter in order to prolong the night and go to bed later and later until it circles back around to early, when the faceless masses are leaving for the office, or are already there. I see them, and I don't want to see myself with them anymore, like all the others, my steps dragging along the metro platforms and corridors and escalators. Forever racing the clock, running red lights, wasting my life. They all look the same in their dark suits and Zara skirts, low heels with flats in their purses. People without smiles, with the pinched faces of city workers, only starting to smile at around one o'clock, when it's time to wolf down a quick sandwich in the park, sitting on the grass, gazing at the sky for a few minutes if it isn't raining. Smiling again during the coffee break, near the machine, the watch giving you the good news: only two more hours to go and it's over. Small life, small joys.

In front of my students, everything changes. Rose Lee has to disappear.

"Madame, is that real?" The girl's voice is coming from the front row, where she always sits.

"No way, she's a teacher! She could never afford a real one!"

I think I know who has spoken, but I don't look up. I pretend I haven't heard. I forgot to switch purses. I should have brought my old, beat-up bag. A few people glanced discreetly at it when I was in the teachers' lounge this morning. My silence and their astonishment. Now I take my lesson plan out of my Chanel bag. I've always dreamed of having one. It's a present from Rose Lee. Only she could have managed it. A nice pair of tits can work miracles, it turns out. I'm absolutely dying to say, "Yes, boys and girls, it's a real one! And?" You'd think the night would give me a little more courage during the day, but right now all I can do is hate myself for being so careless. Fear paralyzes me. My throat is bone-dry. A single teacher could never, ever afford a Chanel purse. As I organize my notes, taking my time before starting class, all I can hear is the girls, their ridiculous, ecstatic murmuring at the sight of the object of our hearts' desire. My nose buried in the syllabus, I feel like I can hear their thoughts. They must suspect a rich lover, that I'm letting myself get screwed in return for pretty post-coital presents. Or maybe they think I'm just a teacher who buys fake Chanel to look fancy.

I try to stop the babble of words, writing on the chalkboard: *We must exercise ourselves in the things which bring happiness, since, if that be present, we have everything, and, if that be absent, all our actions are directed toward attaining it.*

"I'd like to start by analyzing this quote by Epicurus. Focus on the following questions: Am I responsible for my own happiness or unhappiness? Does our happiness come from within us? Can it get away from us? Give examples, please. Think about some examples."

I open the door of the teachers' lounge. People are gathered in a group at the far end of the room, gesturing and talking confusedly. My colleagues' attention has clearly been drawn away from my Chanel bag; they've got better things to do. I join the huddle. In the midst of the group is Martin's young intern, Claire Lopez, whom we recruited based on her results on the teaching aptitude test in French. These days, they can hardly recruit enough people to join the program, much less fill the hundreds of teaching positions available. Result: they're even accepting applicants whose scores are below average. No one wants anything to do with the world's noblest profession anymore. I wonder how much Claire is regretting it. Martin has been very open with me about the girl's struggles to get the students' respect, her problems with them, the humiliation she's been subjected to. She's getting hit in the face with the cold, hard reality of what it means to be a teacher, doesn't yet realize that this could be the only reality everywhere in the national education system. Claire is in absolute hysterics. She's crying real tears, big fat ones, because one of her students—and not just any student, but her *favorite*, the rebellious one who always apologizes, and starts listening again, and learns the lesson (only to forget it almost immediately)—shouted at her, after her umpteenth attempt to bring the class to order, "Suck my dick, bitch!" Claire broke down in front of the whole yelling, babbling class at that point, and the kid stormed out the door.

The assistant principal comes striding into the teachers'

lounge. She places a sheet of paper politely on the table and pushes it toward Claire, who looks up at her questioningly.

"I'd prefer for you to think about this a bit when your head is clearer."

"Think about what?"

"Your complaint."

"Is there a problem with the form?"

"I would strongly encourage you to withdraw it."

"But . . ."

"I know this student quite well. He's not a bad kid."

"Yes, but . . ."

"And—" She leans closer and closer to Claire, so she can speak more quietly—"he's dealing with a very delicate situation at home."

"I understand, but—"

"It's better not to be too harsh, do you see what I'm saying? And I'm even tempted to say"—she leans even closer, her voice no more than a honey-sweet whisper I have to strain to hear—"you're too pretty for that!"

The little group breaks up. The teachers are suddenly late; everyone makes a beeline for his or her pigeonhole, the corridor, the coffee machine, essays that need correcting. Martin arrives just then and heads straight for his intern. The minute I see his face, I know he knows what's happened. He greets Claire sympathetically, says hello to the assistant principal, and hands her back the sheet of paper she put down on the table.

"I think you'd better take this. Mademoiselle Lopez did exactly what one is supposed to do in this type of situation. There's no one in charge of discipline anymore, so we have to react accordingly, wouldn't you say?"

"React? That's not what I'm here for! I'm not a cop!"

"That's not what any of us are here for these days, Madame. That's exactly why you need to take this report and act on it."

The assistant principal closes her mouth, puts Claire's complaint form back down on the table, and leaves the room. Mademoiselle Lopez's ordeal isn't over yet. Martin picks up the form. "I'll deal with it," he tells her.

He leaves arm-in-arm with his intern, giving me a nod. Sometimes I think I spot a glint of lust in his eyes. Like now, with Claire, taking her arm to support her, or console her, maybe. Just a tiny, uncontrollable spark that escapes him like a cry.

5

Elbows propped on the bar, he's with a brunette girl, who only stops laughing long enough to drain glasses of champagne, and two guys. One of them is explaining a cocktail to him:

"You take coffee liqueur, vodka, and . . . milk, if you can believe it—just a couple fingers of milk, you know, not too much—." He shakes his pack of cigarettes like a cocktail shaker. "And then—down the hatch!"

I go over to see them. The one I noticed first is called Cédric. We introduce ourselves, and he starts talking about himself without much prompting. He runs a bar and restaurant near Montmartre. Before he began running his own business, he earned a living as a dancer—and stripper. He talks about the artistic life with sequins in his eyes, and with frankness. All kinds of exchanges went on behind the scenes. Women much older than him often offered him money.

He's young, but he doesn't lack confidence. I leave him just long enough to have my turn on stage and seek him out again immediately afterward, ignoring the crowd and the customers wanting dances. I agree to let Cédric and his friends take me back to my place, where I give myself over to them and the effervescent abandon that follows the night. By seven the next morning, in a café that has just opened, I am so happy. I stay with Cédric and the others, ice cream for me, champagne and cognac for them. I'm not sleepy at all. All I want is to be here where I am, sitting on this café terrace with them, waiting for the time when they'll have to leave for work.

Back at my place, I put the red rose Cédric gave me into a vase. I take money out of my purse, a few business cards, a phone number on a scrap of paper, my makeup kit. Sometimes customers buy red roses from the Indian vendor who comes by selling them and offer them to their dream girls. The flowers are really just an excuse to scribble a few words and a phone number on a bit of paper from a pack of cigarettes, or toilet paper, or a five- or hundred-euro bill. In the wee hours of the morning, the girls go down to the locker room and toss the roses and the notes and the numbers into the trash can. The money, they keep. I get all those things, too: flowers, notes, money. But I keep everything. The notes and business cards end up in a blue box tucked away in my dresser among the t-shirts and underwear.

D.D., sales assistant. J.F., film producer. D.M., attorney at law. P.P., independent wealth management advisor. A.X., car-and-driver rental. F.F., director of sales. V.T., photographer. G.S., dental surgeon. L.S., osteopath. K., physical and mental fitness coach. Etc.

None of these men interest me, or if they do, it's very rarely. It's their numbers that fascinate me, and often their stories. I'm keeping track so that one day I'll be able to look back and remember how many men I met, how many fantasies I was a part of. Because, at night, a man is an open book.

A hasn't touched a woman since his divorce. He doesn't get erections anymore. He's afraid of women, comes here to try and cure himself.

B used to be a gigolo. Now he lives with his dream man. "Women destroyed me," he says.

C loves his wife, goes on and on about his children, shows me photos of his whole family—which doesn't keep him from describing his mistress's body and pussy to me in great detail. He sees her at least once a week.

D is shy. He'll pay for a dance but then doesn't want me to dance. He's only ever been with two women. His dream is to have a little daughter and call her Samia.

E never wants a dance. "I don't like all that stuff," he says, "all these naked bodies." I talk to him about philosophy, and he feels better, tells me he's a medical student, wants to be an ER doctor. "I think I've already seen too many naked bodies," he says. "And the body is sacred."

F has nine kids with four different women. "As far as I know, anyway," he says. "I have one with a call girl. I know a lot of women like you."

G is an ardent admirer of Spinoza. At first he doesn't believe I'm a philosophizing stripper. Or a stripping philosopher. But it makes him want to lick my pussy even more. He stayed faithful to his wife for nine years, but then she stopped taking care of him. Now he's got four mistresses in different cities around the world (he travels a lot). He wears a cashmere suit. Bespoke. Seven thousand euros.

J says, "This is the dream. You ask your wife, 'Honey, would you put on a sexy little dress and strip for me?' and you get hit in the face with an iron!"

K is crazy in love with Poppy. He got married last month, and his wife has already called him twelve times in one evening! He says she's a ballbuster. He wants to tell her to go fuck herself.

L says that, out in the real world, a woman like the ones who dance here would never speak to him. Other girls, the kind men meet on the street, in regular life, can't compare. He's never touched women as perfect as us.

M says, "Can you please tell me what on earth I was thinking? I shouldn't have come here; it's too amazing. Do you realize you're every guy's number one fantasy?"

N spent more than fifteen years in the army. He knows the Amazon rainforest like the back of his hand because he was stationed there for a lot of that time. Three years of war in Yugoslavia; he didn't think men were capable of such savagery. Now he works in logging in the Amazon and respects the trees. You don't cut down a tree unless it's eighty years old. He likes to have his nipples fondled.

O blubbers: "I don't want to get hard! No, I don't want to! What will you think of men? We're all alike, filthy macho pigs. Horny pervs. I don't want to offend you. Getting an erection here is disrespectful!"

P wants me to wear pantyhose. He wants to rip them off. Offers to pay for two hours in a private room.

Q says he can't take it anymore. His wife won't suck him off anymore, won't have sex with him. He's forced to see prostitutes just to feel a little bit like a man. "I need someone to take care of me!" he cries in my ear.

R wants more. I tell him I won't do any more. "Why won't you do that? I don't get it. What difference does it make? It's all the same stuff, right?" "No, dancing is *not* the same as letting myself be licked or penetrated." "But I'll pay you a lot of money!" "It's not about the money." "Then what's it about? What else is there, other than money?"

S says, "I'm going to be honest with you. You make me hard as hell. Just tell me how much you want, doesn't matter. You're a real woman. You make me so hot. I can satisfy you; I'm hung like a horse. I'm gonna lick you all over, I swear." He's twenty-two.

T hides his fantasy in a suitcase stashed away in the basement. Latex skirts, size 10 stilettos, chains. Every so often he'll say he's going out with the guys, but really he goes to S&M parties. He's looking for a mistress, a dominatrix. He's been married for twelve years. His wife doesn't suspect a thing.

U says, "I love it when those nipples get hard! Is that for me? Do I make you wet? Is that it? I like big clits, too, a little meat there, know what I mean? Big lips . . . Hey, you got any dope?"

V was often punished by his mother when he was little. Spankings, his tears, and the hand groping for *maman*'s underwear beneath her skirt. The smell of his mother's sex, his most precious memory.

W has never confessed his true sexual desires to his wife. He's got enough money to pay professionals to sodomize him.

X enjoys touching a woman's armpits when she's sweating. That's what he likes, to make love to a woman after her workout.

Y wants me to say sweet things to him, like I'm in love with him, and to look into his eyes, no dancing. An expression on my face that says, "I love you."

Z sits perfectly still while I'm dancing. And then he cries. "It's impossible," he says to me. "A man can't be with only one woman."

Men. Letters of an alphabet I never knew, but I want to know it now. I see now that men do talk about love, and it's also their words that intoxicate me: *"You have the face of love . . . I wish I could be the pole when you dance onstage . . . You frighten me . . . If I were a beautiful woman, I would do the same thing as you—make men get hard . . . You're a thief; you stole that smile from heaven . . . Is there any way I could buy one of your G-strings from you? . . . The most frustrating thing isn't that I don't possess you, it's that you do this for me without knowing me . . . Is this the way you really are when you make love? . . . What you do should be covered by health insurance . . . Do you mind if I touch myself? . . . I wish my wife would do this for me at home . . . How many tickets would it cost for me to come? . . . May I kiss your feet? . . . If I were a woman, I'd be a whore . . . You're just a one-night dream! I don't have the right to fall in love with you . . . I'm not sentimental about women; they're horrible . . . What are you doing next weekend? I know a really beautiful church. Want to get married?"*

*

Amidst the night's jumble of male voices, I sometimes feel the need to detach myself, to look in from the outside at the carnival, the endless whirling of the carousel, the tizzy of the skirt-chasers, the clowns' capers versus their habitual ennui, the naked acrobats. The poles to which we cling like the pillars of time, and the never-ending spectacle. The coat-check girls coming round in an infinite loop to take the jackets of the dazzled men turning in circles, credit cards in hand. Here, the end of time is always pushed back to tomorrow, and while we wait, we dance.

In that whole faceless crowd, there is only one being that makes me wonder. He comes here often, a tireless partier who raises his glass like a victorious gesture. Dozens of victories, all of which he knocks back the same way, methodically, with no apparent pleasure or displeasure. He acts at home here, sometimes going up on stage, without anyone on staff batting an eyelash. He imitates the dancers, strikes lascivious poses, sometimes giving himself a little spanking. His hair is longish, and he twirls it around his fingers. Two enormous, limpid green bruises dominate his face: impossible to say if they're really eyes. A gaze whose emptiness you can get lost in. I don't dare approach him, even though something in me desperately wants to. Occasionally a girl will go up to him, hoping for a dance, but without success. Others just stare at him in astonishment, retreating into a silence of incomprehension or distaste. He's a forgotten being, forgetting himself in a bottle, in the confusion of his actions, and always after two o'clock in the morning.

He is the one, this man with his disturbing beauty, who is beginning to inhabit my nights, in which all the others are becoming sadly ordinary.

6

I'm meeting up with Martin in half an hour. I'm exhausted, but I promised we'd see each other after his academic inspection. It was this morning; I hope it went well for him. I make myself another coffee, my fourth today, I think. Without sugar, the coffee from the machine has a musty taste that never fails to wake me up. It rises up into my brain before drifting back down and dissipating in the cold water I chase it with. Quickly now, walk a few steps. Moving around wakes me up, too. I only slept three hours last night. All I can see in the ladies' room mirror are the black circles under my eyes. I apply another layer of makeup, but I don't think anything can hide the excitement of my sleepless nights or my rapidly multiplying crows' feet. Today I've got a copy of Alessandro Baricco's *Mr. Gwyn* for Martin (he's already read *Ocean Sea* and *Novecento*). It gives us something to talk about. Without him, there's no question that I'd be absolutely lost at school. Kind of like today. I was so tired this morning that I forgot my packed lunch, which means I have to eat in the cafeteria. I head there like a beast to the slaughterhouse. The food looks utterly depressing on the plywood tables with their blunted corners, chipped carafes, and small glasses, overcooked pasta without salt. Teachers and students clench their ass-cheeks so they won't fall off the tiny chairs they're balanced on. It's like one enormous, chewing jaw, this mass of humanity crushing any zeal, any enthusiasm along with its food. Nothing scares me more than the thought of becoming like them.

Sitting here in this high school cafeteria, we are nothing but women and men brought together in an obscene display of our lack of drive and passion. Our faces and our speech are empty of any intensity. I never stop hoping to surprise my colleagues in the act of showing some life—anger or joy, it doesn't matter, as long as it's something *alive*. Judging them soothes me, in my smallness. Because, of course, I'm different from all those simpletons who think they've already won the battle of nobility against poverty of mind and are now content simply to let themselves drift down the long, lazy river of self-satisfaction. *Congratulations*, I think, disdainfully. They've never even thought about real happiness. There it is; that's the reality they're serving up in this room, on a plastic plate. I eat my scorn while I watch my colleagues swallowing, swallowing it all down, talking about students and methods, planning and staff meetings. They're thrilled about the additional hour that'll bring a little extra money at the end of the month. They've already got stacks of papers under their arm to correct on the train or the metro. I look away so I won't have to participate in their conversations, reassuring myself that I'm not like them, taking refuge in thoughts directed toward the open spaces, the trees in the gardens. A window can be enough to save your life. I pretend not to hear Stéphane, sitting across from me, talking with his colleagues about whether it's possible to instill perfect egalitarianism in French schools: "We have to get rid of everything but the essential subjects. Don't you think, Jo?"

In asking me the question, he forces me to turn toward him and the others.

"What exactly is an essential subject, Stéphane?"

"Well, biology is essential, for example. It's universal. All of humanity has a share in it, you know, this knowledge . . ."

"So we should teach music, but not French? English but not French history?"

"Good points," observes Martin, who has just appeared.

"The end of teaching is nigh, in any case. We're doomed to extinction; didn't you know? If what my intern says is to be believed, soon there will be nothing left but trainers and technicians."

He gives me a kiss on the cheek and motions for me to come away with him.

"How did the inspection go?"

"Really well, as far as I'm concerned. I taught the class exactly the way I wanted to, as always."

"Ah, I see, you stuck to the classics."

"Yes, the inspector did get on my case a bit, for a certain lack of originality. See, literature isn't original, apparently, and what she referred to as 'abusing the classics' just isn't exciting enough. She reminded me that it's 'important to open schooling up to all forms of culture, without any exclusions.' And why didn't I use comics? Because 'we have to embrace the cultural practices of the students,' she says, 'and from that perspective, content and materials are beside the point. *Star Trek* or Proust, it's the same thing, if it'll make them work without too much effort . . . it's your responsibility to put yourself at their level . . .'"

"Well, here we are, Martin. The time has come when we have to learn from the learners, the era of the new liberal-libertarian European school, conveniently reliant on the persistent saintliness of teachers in the service of the child-king."

"Exactly. At one point I called out a kid who was slumping sideways in his chair, maybe about to fall—he was half-asleep. And you know what she said to me? That we should 'make sure they can express their spontaneity.' She said she was unclear about what 'skill' I'd been trying to 'enable' in my students, and then she went off on this endless tangent about ways of acquiring knowledge, but then, of course, she *also* wanted to make sure I understood that 'it isn't knowledge that counts, but enabling skills.' She went on and on about the sacrosanct use of images. I couldn't stop myself from telling her that kids' minds these days are already crippled by way too many simulacra."

"You actually had the balls to say that?"

"Yeah, but she cut me off fast to remind me that I'm here to do what I'm asked to do, even if I don't like it; I'm here to show them 'the right images' because they illustrate obscure ways of thinking that are otherwise inaccessible, because 'it's not easy to read André Gide, and even for us as educated adults, plays are often daunting and don't lend themselves to being read.' I mean, how the hell am I supposed to feel after that?"

"Martin, I get it, it's not easy to force ourselves to take things for what they aren't. The only way is to kill off a little part of ourselves."

"Well, look. I'd better get back to my grading and my oh-so-saintly job. Didn't Kant say it was impossible to be immoral in doing one's duty?"

"He absolutely did."

Then I add, "Wait—I haven't put it in your pigeonhole yet, but here's your present. Baricco."

"Thanks, Jo. What would we do without this stuff?"

Martin kisses me on the cheek and takes the book, squeezing my hand. I watch him walk away, bringing the hand he squeezed up to my nostrils. I think I like his scent. I think I'd like to press my body against his, too. But how can I tell this respectable man of letters that I put my ass on display several nights a week, to make men get hard so they'll give me lots of money? The discrepancy flashes through my mind in all its crudeness. Martin wouldn't like Rose Lee. She'd awaken the pig inside him, the one he stifles with poetry. I caught him staring at my chest once. Just once. I liked it. But Martin will only yield to the temptation of angels, talks only about "saintly sighs" and "the cries of the fairies." He clings to metaphor and euphemism to escape the ugliness of the world. It's hard to imagine him giving way to animal sensuality. And yet . . . the poet, too, buckles under the weight of the burden he carries between his legs. That's all literature talks about. What if he saw me, nearly naked onstage? Maybe he wouldn't even recognize me. Rose Lee's eyes are dark with kohl and mascara. She changes her hair, uses extensions, wears it down. Rose Lee wears a corset. Her skin is velvety, her back arched, her breasts voluptuously revealed. Rose Lee could be a thousand other women. She isn't me.

I quickly go to collect my things and stow away the copy of a new teaching manual sent by a publishing house so I can get home. There's a green envelope in my pigeonhole, on top of a pile of administrative papers.

Drancy, December 10, 2005

Dear Madame,

Thank you—your reply was great! You made me so happy, you don't even know. I wasn't sure if I should write you. I have a problem, but I can't talk to my friends about it. I can't tell them I'm interested in philosophy to solve my problems. I know I don't need to explain it to you, you understand everything.

You say philosophy taught you that there are ideas that can save us. What ideas are those, Madame? I've read your letter over and over again, but I don't understand. But you can help me, I know it. So what the hell. Two years ago, I was in tenth grade with a girl named Anne. She and her family moved, and she transferred to another school, near Sceaux, I think. We were really good friends; she helped me with my schoolwork a lot. You can probably guess the rest. Except there is no rest, and that's the problem. I think I like her, but I've never been able to work up the guts to tell her. She intimidated me too much. And I was a coward, and I didn't even go to her going-away party. I'm so mad at myself. I've been mad at myself for two whole years. What can philosophy do for that? I just can't see it at all.

    Thank you, Madame.

Hadrien

* * *

Paris, December 12, 2005

Dear Hadrien,

You've made my day! And I'm a bit flattered, too, I'll admit. If my letter made you feel enthusiastic and made you want to go further, I'm very glad to take some time for you and try to give you some concrete answers, this time, for the problems you're dealing with.

    Philosophy speaks in concepts. More radically, philosophy is the creation of concepts. Its way of moving forward is abstract; it doesn't speak directly to "life stuff." What it attempts to do, rather, is theorize about those things. To get straight to the heart of real things, reading literature might be a better bet. There's no better education. But let's talk about philosophy! Let's think about your problem. You're suffering from regret: at not confessing your love, not acting to find out whether your feelings were mutual. I know how hard that can be. Maybe you can forget—but are we truly capable of making ourselves forget? I don't believe so. In reading your letter, a very beautiful saying from a Stoic philosopher leapt to my mind first thing. Marcus Aurelius, remember him? We've talked about him in class. He said, "We do not control what happens; we merely control how we respond to it." Right now, you're feeling as if you've failed: "I should have, but I didn't." So be it. Yet, if we reflect on the meaning of Marcus Aurelius's words, we can see that you have two options available to you. First, the past is past, and you can't *control it anymore, but the choice is yours whether to accept that or not. In other words, if you refuse to accept what you didn't do, you're adding anger to your regret. Accepting it means exercising the power of your own free will over your thoughts and soothing the regret and sadness that go along with those thoughts. Second, though you can't change the past, you can act on the present, not only through reflection, but also with action. In other words, it isn't too late to get in touch with Anne and ask to meet up with her, or whatever you like. When action is possible, it's a way of exercising our power over the course of events, and thus over our lives. The consequences of action can't always be predicted and aren't entirely within your control (which is why you have to think carefully, to engage in the work of reflection, you might say). But you do have the power, right here and now, to accept the past or not, and to act now, or not.*

    Sincerely,

Josephine

7

A ndrea's assigned me a newly freed-up locker. It's like a promotion: Rose Lee's name is up in the dressing room. I peeled off the sticker with Electra's name on it, the one who got herself fired. She'd tried to disable the camera in one of the private rooms. Electra had forgotten that the eye never stops watching us. Some dancers are tempted, sometimes, to promise clients what they can't give them. Fleur didn't like Electra; this wasn't the first time she'd seen her break the rules. "It's what she deserved," she told me. "She was stupid, and she got caught."

I've been Rose Lee for about a month now. Not bad for someone who never should have even started this job, and now keeps putting off her resignation. I started. I kept going. And the problem now is that I'm starting to get emotionally involved here. Having a locker means you're part of the family. It touches me. And besides, I've decided to allow myself to keep dancing through the holiday vacation. It's been forever since I could take advantage of the semiannual sales in January. I need boots, a coat, sheets, a desk lamp, and new glasses. I'd like to go on a trip during the February break. Somewhere exotic, sunny in the middle of winter, with a new bathing suit. The top floor of Galeries Lafayette has an huge range of bathing suits to choose from all year round. That's luxury, too—sunshine, twelve months of the year. All those things a humble little civil servant could never afford, unless they've opted for a career as an expatriate teacher in Tahiti or

Mauritius or the Caribbean. I make more money than an expatriate teacher, but I'm not actually allowed to. Civil servants cannot combine public-sector employment with paid private work. It's called "obligation to exclusive exercise of function." Law no. 83-634, effective July 13, 1983. It's categorical. Last month I rented a safety-deposit box at my bank. I don't put anything but two-hundred- and five-hundred-euro notes in it. I love making those little yellow and pink bundles; it gives me goosebumps every time. The pleasure is incomparable, but I know it won't last. In addition to tips, I get paid a salary via bank transfer. And that's proof of other employment. That's the unambiguous reality that will show up on my tax return. I'll be required to stop. It's not sustainable, the vast difference between day and night, the public sector and the private. Rose Lee is going to end up trapping Jo. I've been thinking about a career change for years—but, other than teaching, what can I be with a master's degree in philosophy? A stripper?

I've decided to give myself a little more time. Tonight I'm wearing that beautiful transparent black dress and flouting the so-called obligation to morality: "In his or her private life, the civil servant is required to behave in a manner that conveys dignity and must never display an attitude that risks shocking others." Bit obtrusive, that civil servitude. Hand in hand with Fleur, I go upstairs.

It's Sharon's turn onstage. Fleur whispers in my ear: "Have you seen her new ass yet? Remember? She was so gross with that paunch—can you imagine gaining weight just so they can inject the fat into your ass? What are these bitches gonna do when big asses aren't trendy anymore?"

"Maybe it'll deflate."

"Chicks like that don't deflate."

A customer calls Fleur over, and she walks away. It's beginning early tonight. I look for Poppy, so we can start out together. We're stronger in pairs; it gives us the courage to flirt with customers, even without drinking. We sit down at tables without being invited. That's how the game works here. The men like it; it saves them from having to make the first move. And here, the first move isn't some covert operation. We trade roles, and everything becomes simpler, communication is much clearer, we're all finally speaking the same language. Sometimes we're partners in crime, one held hostage by his own desire, the other seized by the giddiness of seduction.

Being that woman means playing with a man. Offering him the dream, but being the only one to capitalize on it. He believes her, she lets him. He asks, she stalls. He has expectations, she walks away. Sometimes he pays a lot of money for her just to make conversation with him, smiling while she drinks his bottle of champagne. At other times, he thinks he's buying something. "I'm paying you," he says. Yes, he's paying her for the pleasure of not having her. And it will be incredible; she's the one who's promised him that. He sits down, steeling himself not to come, and asks her for more and more bliss, because she is a professional who will bend over backwards to give him endless pleasure. But it doesn't come cheap. He pays not to touch. He pays not to see. He pays not to have it. He'll empty his bank account for her. The stripper, and the oblivion. Worse than a prostitute. But when he goes home, he's comforted. The bed is warm; his wife is sleeping. And he has had the dream. It was real, like the pleasure of jerking off in the bathroom. He's pleased with himself for not actually having done anything. He hasn't cheated on his wife. No, he hasn't.

The circle is complete. The show is over.

But it will start again, endlessly.

He will come back, to drink in the sight of the dancer, facing the mirror in which she is who she has always wanted to be. As a woman. As a man. When the woman dances, it's always herself she's dancing with. That pleasure can't be shared; it's hers alone, untransmittable. But he thinks, out there in the audience, that she's dancing for him. Sometimes he even thinks that she desires him, or that she's fallen in love with him. The illusion is so perfect that he'd rather believe she's lying when she denies it sweetly. The truth is that she's driving him to romanticize, to fantasize, to pay for her future vacations and her new clothes and her silk sheets. Both of them are hiding behind that curtain in the private room, their pleasure out of sight.

I start my night off with a banker who likes to read poetry. He regrets not having followed his dream in life of doing what he loves most: reading, writing, and flying. He didn't want to burden his parents with the cost of earning a pilot's license, so he chose caution, security. He's thinking of quitting his job. But no, he can't. He's about to become a father. The baby is due next week. "I'm not married," he keeps repeating. "No, I'm not married."

At around two A.M., I go down to the dressing room for my snack. When I come back upstairs, I think I spot the man with the green eyes, but it isn't him. Something's nagging at me. I don't want to trawl for any more dances or money tonight. Cédric's arrival is providential. I fling my arms around him.

"You're here to rescue me! Thank you!"

"I don't know what I'm rescuing you from, but don't disappear. I want to watch you—alone."

At closing time, I follow him without hesitation.

Later, I call the principal's secretary to say I'm not going to be at school. I decide to start my vacation a day early. My scruples vanish entirely at the prospect of having some fun. Right now, everything seems clear. Joséphine, that little coward, is seeking her redemption. I'm still Rose Lee with Cédric, even after the night, without my heels or costume, but still ready to party. We go to his restaurant, which is brimful of music, the kitchen clattering with good food and cakes coming out of the ovens. We drink champagne and eat salad, and he prepares some filet of beef with black pepper—an improvised recipe that's his remedy for the exhaustion of the night. And I have nothing to do except indulge myself. To be Rose Lee, stopping the sunrise, prolonging the night, the day. To be with him every morning, as long as our mutual pleasure lasts. Rose Lee, giving herself up to Cédric's kisses. Rose Lee, lingering with him in his bed in the flat behind the kitchen, waking up to the smell of the warm croissants he brings for her. The customers are already there; I meet the chef's knowing gaze and sit down at the table right next to the counter. My new place in life. I gaze at Cédric, my whole body straining toward his caress.

He serves me a strong coffee.

Some of the girls have warned me never to turn around if someone calls out my stage name in the street. To avoid being recognized, they hide behind sunglasses—which they wear even in winter—or beneath hats, muffled up in scarves. No more sequins. No more mask. Drawn, unglamorous faces, one last cigarette between their lips. They head for their cars or for a taxi, eager to get home, on the nights they haven't changed into clubwear to keep the party going. I've sometimes fallen asleep with my makeup still on, taught my first few classes with glitter stuck to my cheeks, run my fingers through my hair and smiled at men passing on the street. I explore my body the way you would a new lover's. I am putty in my own hands. I hated this body for so long, but now it's my personal celebration. And not only when I use my charms on men only too happy to succumb to them, or when I'm beneath the lights, facing the mirrors and that perfect illusion. It's my body, only mine. It isn't without flaws, but Rose Lee has made it desirable. She has what it takes to bestow pleasure and drive away shame. Something only men like. I've let Jo fall away along with my clothing. I pushed moral order to the cliff's edge, and it fell and smashed, and deservedly so. For me, the most beautiful fall is the waterfall of my hair cascading down my back. I mean, fuck it! Finally I can say, fuck it all! Fuck the cafeteria, fuck seriousness, fuck the students, fuck standardization. Fuck Descartes! The body isn't a thing, but the thing that thinks. And above all, above *all*, fuck always being so well-spoken. I can permit myself to be light and lowbrow. I don't intellectualize everything anymore, because that'll make a hard cock wilt. Rose Lee doesn't need a master's degree. I became Rose Lee so that culture wouldn't be the instrument of my own lies anymore. I became her to stop hiding myself behind a pair of cotton panties with little pink flowers, pubic hair poking out like weeds. What will my desires be if I'm only Jo, with her big jugs, unable to look away from her love-handles? This stomach sheathed in a corset is no longer Jo's. And neither is this hairless pussy. We're finally looking each other in the eye, her and me, our gazes meeting in the mirror. I used to allow my pussy to be looked at, but I never wanted to see it. I couldn't make out the rosy flesh, the folds of the little lips, the way they were beautifully asymmetrical. But now I know my pussy well, and I love it. I'd love to show it to all the men I encounter during the nights. I wax it a few times a week, sometimes every other day. My skin has never been so smooth. I've never bought so many disposable razors, exfoliating scrubs, body creams, hand creams, foot creams, face creams, hair products.

At home, I dance naked, with or without music. I occupy my own body because it is me, my stomach, my thighs, my arms. And the pussy and the ass, those are me, too. I'm not naked when I'm nude, anymore. I'm a complete being. I strike Rose Lee's poses in front of the mirror and stare at myself, astonished. I spread my legs, to possess myself. I part the lips and slide a fingertip inside my moistness and taste myself. It's my taste. It's me. I slap my own ass. One slap, and then a caress. My life has the softness of my skin, the exuberance of my breasts. Before, I was just dragging my carcass around. I only thought of my body when I was trying to forget that I had one, when I was trying to erase it beneath clothes that were too big, hiding my legs, flattening my chest. Always exhausted, pins and needles all over, the spreading tentacles of inertia. My body was trying to escape, it had stopped belonging to me. Just a lump, an abscess that swells and swells and ends up exploding.

8

I'm not a lesbian, not at all, but honestly, I've totally fallen for you. I've been watching you. You've made so much progress since you started here. You should be coming in more often; the customers are always asking to see Rose Lee. If I were a man, I'd want to marry you. Come on, let's have a drink."

Iris takes me by the hand. We worked together last night, at the same table, midway through the evening. That's how you get to know the other girls, at a table with customers. It helps me understand better what they expect from the strippers. I watch the other girls. There's a lot to learn from the way they act. Iris, for example, deploys her charms with the spontaneity of a child, but every move is actually shrewdly calculated. She figures out each customer's personality very quickly and puts herself on the same level.

Iris is an actress. She dances at night to make some money and keep her membership in the stage actors' union. Almost no one in her life knows about her nocturnal activities. She takes full advantage of the job; being a stripper allows her to play all kinds of different roles, and understanding the men helps her to understand herself better. She came to Paris to work, but her family lives near Metz, and she goes back regularly to take care of her hedgehogs. She and her sister have set up a little refuge—Iris likes to call it a hospital—for the critters they find and nurse back to health. One day, when she's got a lot of money, she's going to open a hedgehog rescue center.

At the bar, we wait for Ariane to pour us the first drink of the night.

"So, how's it going with Fleur?"

"With Fleur? What do you mean?"

"Oh, everybody can tell what's going on; we get it. And we know Fleur! She's crazy about you! Are you bi?"

"I like men."

"Men, sure. Look, here comes one now."

The guy approaches the bar. He's thirtyish and tentative, standing very straight in his gray suit. His white shirt is wrinkled. He scans the room with his shifting gaze and finally dares to look at the stage, searching for a glimpse of ass and then quickly looking down. His slight lazy eye does nothing to conceal his shame. He's walking on eggshells.

Iris arches her back slightly, the fingers of one hand trailing over her cleavage.

"Watch this," she whispers in my ear. "He's one of those shy late bloomers who likes a girl to be forward."

"Hey there, you," she purrs to him. "Wanna kiss, or should we get straight to licking each other?"

The man doesn't speak. He turns his back to us and orders a drink.

"Don't worry; this is normal," she murmurs. "He'll bite, you'll see."

Smoothing her palms over her breasts, she approaches the customer again. While she's trying to get his attention, the green-eyed man arrives and sits in his usual spot.

I pull Iris toward me.

"Who is he?"

"Who? That guy over there?"

"Do you know him?"

She turns away from the customer, who is finally working up the nerve to talk to her, and says to me, her tone impatient now:

"Don't bother. All the girls like him, not that he does anything to deserve it. He's not normal. I've never seen him with a girl."

"What's his name?"

I'm irritating her with my questions. I've interrupted her game. I think she's mad at me; she steps away abruptly, tossing the name "Thomas" over her shoulder. The customer offers to buy her a drink. Iris was right. He's a shy late bloomer who likes a girl to be forward.

Thomas, then. I try to figure out how long I've been seeing him here, in the VIP area, sitting in the same place. Has he always been there? Normally, I never approach customers sitting at reserved tables. They buy magnums of this or that, bottles costing more than a thousand euros, profligate with champagne and intoxications of all sorts. I don't like such conspicuous displays of wealth and luxury. I watch them from a distance, with no desire to be the instrument of their pointless gratification. But for the past few weeks, my eyes have been going in that direction more and more often. I don't remember exactly when the first time was. Thomas is a vague impression, his face melting into the night and sometimes reappearing during the day, a blur. When he's there, I watch him, night and weariness on his face. Vulnerability concealed behind alcohol and indifference. Between drinks, customers, dances, I often pause, hoping to see him, sitting there in his spot. Past the wide lobby staircase, past the ticket window and the cashier, past the dressing room stairs, the door opens and closes thousands of times every night. Being here means waiting for him, just a little.

Ariane calls me, but I don't want a drink anymore. I go down into the dressing room and surprise Fleur, peeing behind the half-open bathroom door. She winks at me. "Are you watching me, you vixen?" she says. Her face is lined with fatigue, but she doesn't want to tell me what she's been doing instead of sleeping. "To sleep is to die," she says, dodging the question. "I've been living." I don't push it. She offers to let me try her new lipstick. Pressed against my side at the mirror, she nudges me and murmurs, low: "You seen the chick? The new one? Poppy told me she made a thousand euros cash on top of her pay. Big tits, sweetie, big tits—and stupid. Blows my mind."

"May I remind you that I've got big tits, too? Not *that* big, but . . ."

"But you don't have a brain the size of a marble, sweetie."

We hear the dressing-room door slam. Andrea's in a rage. We're about to be treated to an emphatic reminder of the rules. No one speaks. Andrea has one of the dancers sit down in a chair, demonstrates a couple of dance steps, and recaps the restrictions that are clearly outlined and posted in the dressing rooms:

"Employees must comply with the following rules . . . no physical contact with the clientele. *'To all dancers. IMPOR-TANT!!! We remind you that physical contact during private dances is strictly forbidden by French law. In other words, NO TOUCHING of the customers. Thank you for your coopera-tion.'*"

I go upstairs with Fleur, knowing we're going to have to be extremely careful tonight. I'm planning to allocate tonight's earnings to my next purchase. I saw the most beautiful stilet-tos in a boutique on the Champs-Élysées, and I've been dreaming of wearing them. They're the kind of shoes that make a woman feel privileged to be a woman. That was part of the reason I decided to work over the whole Christmas vacation from school. To treat myself to some luxury, and a few souvenirs of the time when I was Rose Lee. But there are more important things in the main room tonight than my new heels. Thomas is still there, alone at his table, with his mag-num and the still-empty glasses. He lifts a hand to shoulder height, fingers playing across imaginary piano keys. Did he just give me a sideways glance? I take two steps, three, and stop in front of those dancing hands. His fingers stop fluttering, and he holds out a hand to me and invites me to have a drink with him.

Sitting next to him—I've never been this close to him—I talk without knowing what to say, searching my mind for words I can string together that will make me sound clever or amusing. The smile I plaster on my face is forced, like it's catching on something somewhere. I cough instead of speaking, cover my mouth while my eyes search desperately for help, scan the room, simulate surprise. What's happening over there? Is someone calling me? I'm tempted to get up and flee. Except that absolutely nothing is happening over there, and no one is calling Rose Lee. I'm scared, that's what's going on. I look around the room again. Where are Iris and Fleur? Why aren't they with me? Iris must be with her late bloomer; I saw them heading for the ticket-window not too long ago. Fleur, I have no idea. All I can do is drain my glass in one swallow; the alcohol will help. Thomas doesn't make any effort to keep the conversation flowing. I'm sure he thinks I'm new here, incapable of enticing a customer.

"My name's Rose Lee."

The words come out of my mouth like a belch. Finally, relief. Telling him my name is a start, isn't it? He smiles and refills my empty glass, then raises his own in a toast. We drink while we wait for the words that will come along with drunkenness. The DJ approaches the table to shake his hand. Thomas hands him a brimming glass and whispers something in his ear. Wink, thump on the shoulder. I don't know what's happening. All I know is that the seat I'm sitting in, holding a glass of champagne and wearing the outfit of a cheap courtesan, isn't mine anymore. Thomas sets his glass down next to the ice bucket, pushes the table away slightly with his foot, and invites me to do what I'm here to do. Dance for him. Strip. Arms resting along the back of the sofa, he tilts his head back and spreads his legs so I can get very close to him. He knows how to arrange his body for a dance, but I don't want to dance anymore. I gyrate without desire, sway without believing it. I slide between him and the table and adjust my G-string before settling myself astride his lap and slipping off my dress. I look deeply into his eyes, which is what I really want to do, deflowering him gently with my gaze, slowly, taking my time, savoring this endless moment, this unique moment, the first one, that only happens once in a lifetime. I don't take off my bra, but I seek out his lips. I kiss him, tangling my tongue with his. There it is, that thing we were trying to say.

"Bravo," he murmurs. "That seems real."

"Maybe it is . . ."

He suggests, uncertainly, that I come and find him when I've finished work.

"Not tonight. Another time. When you're not drunk."

He laughs, lets his head fall back, starts playing the piano with his fingers again. It's his silent music, suspended in the emptiness of his alcohol-filled nights, and he tells me no, there's no way, drunkenness is his shadow, without it he would disappear. He plunges a hand into his pocket and pulls out a five-hundred-euro note, which he crumples like a receipt and stuffs into my hand. I clench my fist. He stands up while I get dressed, and I whisper in his ear that I'm working next Wednesday. "What's your name?" I ask, but he's already walking away. I feel like I didn't have time to accomplish anything; I stay there, sitting in the spot he's left, feeling like I've failed at something. I unclench my fist: it really is five hundred euros. I set it on the table and smooth it with my hand. I'm going to buy those shoes. They'll be a gift from Thomas. Now we know each other, he and I. Maybe, one day.

Yes, but what day, when there is only the night?

*

He comes back Wednesday night. Maybe for me, but without his shadow, with its absence. He seems perfectly sober. I catch a glimpse of him between two private room sessions. I cut short my dance and cash out the customer so I can go and talk to him. I run toward the abyss. He's already gone.

9

S unday, already.

No more panic. Since I've been living this endless weekend, I don't dread Mondays anymore. Not only is it the school holidays, but Monday's my day off, like it is for all artists. Mondays used to give me migraines. Nausea, just from setting the alarm.

At four-thirty in the morning, among the few customers still dotted around the place, I recognize one of Thomas's friends. I go up to him without hesitation. "Hi, how are you? You're a regular, aren't you? What's your name?" Always the same words to get the conversation going. He buys me a drink. Jean-Philippe has a kind of old-fashioned elegance, a disdainful detachment, like, "Nothing can affect me, because I'm untouchable and always will be—so you can go to hell." He wears cashmere and Weston loafers. He slips me a hundred-euro tip and invites me to come for one last drink at the home of some friends of his. Thomas might be there, so I'd like to go. But Fleur doesn't want to come with me; she'd rather go to another afterparty. I watch her getting ready in the dressing room, redoing her makeup, chattering excitedly with Poppy. I put on a fresh coat of lipstick and head out alone to the address Jean-Philippe gave me.

I'm disappointed from the moment I walk in the door. This isn't a party, just an icily opulent orgy, with two girls Jean-Philippe invited for his friend Ben, who owns the apartment. Slumped on a couch, his gaze lost in hopelessness, Ben is just staring into space. He's depressed; his wife has left him. Jean-Philippe thinks he's being a good friend: cocaine, alcohol, prostitutes. I want to leave. There's no point in my being here, but they bring out a bottle of Cristal Roederer, just for me. Jean-Philippe makes himself right at home. He's authoritative. You'd think he was in charge, master of the house.

"Are you sure you want to open that bottle?"

Sometimes I forget myself. I ask stupid questions without thinking; the pleb in me comes out, worried about wasting. The virtuousness of the not-so-well-born. But how can I not see the waste? Their extravagance makes me cringe. And yet I can't deny the truth: luxury is bliss. It's so nice not to give a fuck; that's one of the pleasures my second identity has allowed me to experience. Undreamt-of orgasms. Sometimes I feel like I'm licking up the crumbs they let fall with tact and caution. Could their waste be a calculated move?

I say yes to a glass of Cristal.

Ben summons the last dregs of his wherewithal and rises, heroic and dignified, to offer me a tour of his princely apartment. Showing off his wealth boosts his spirits a bit. I contemplate the Jacuzzi. He tells me about all the parties he throws, says that Thomas—"You know Thomas, right?"—has gone in there naked more than once. I drop my gaze and don't say anything. The bathroom trash can is sterling silver. He pulls open his wife's dresser drawers, crammed with lingerie, and takes out a few items, suggesting that I try them on.

I say no to Chantal Thomass.

The two girls are starting to get restless. They eye the bedroom and the super king-size bed while Ben stays glued to my side, takes me by the arm, refills my glass. Right under our noses, without being asked to do it, the girls start to fondle and undress one another. Their eyes are hungry, their movements clearly practiced, like two machines. Their greed disgusts me, and their faces distorted by lying, their poorly cobbled-together act. There's nothing erotic about it. It's all just a cheap show.

Arm in arm with Ben, I'm almost taller than him. I hate being taller than a man. I need to feel like I can be physically dominated. I let my arm drop to my side, freeing myself from his embrace, pretending I need the bathroom. The two whores take advantage of the moment to lead him into the bedroom.

Back in the living room, I sit down next to Jean-Philippe and pick up my glass of champagne. I proceed to drown myself in it while he reminisces pleasurably about the more memorable parties that have been held here. Amid these four hundred square meters of marble sculptures, long hallways, hot tubs and high ceilings, it's clearer than ever to me that Paris's endless metro-job-bed treadmill most of us are stuck on is a shit deal. We slave away like dogs while others, to forget their petty little sorrows, have bitches in heat make house calls. Who's the prostitute? The answer's not entirely clear to me. Before I've even finished this fresh glass of champagne (I've learned to measure time in emptied glasses), I see Ben running toward us with little hopping steps, like a child's. He's still got his white shirt on, but he's bare-assed, the little pink head of his dick flopping around. He starts blubbering and clings to me on the sofa, legs curled beneath him. I don't know what to say. Jean-Philippe doesn't bat an eyelash. I suppose all of this is perfectly normal. The girls come back out into the living room, too, of course. I don't find them any more beautiful without clothes on. One of them grips Ben's ankles so he'll stretch his legs out on the sofa, while the other lifts his shirt, exposing his penis, and gets right down to business, swallowing a mouthful of soft flesh in the hope of reviving it. Her partner keeps a firm hold on Ben's ankles, while he clutches my arm even more tightly, making sharp little noises that aren't sounds of pleasure. The bobbing mouth reveals intermittent glimpses of wrinkled skin. The girl holding Ben's ankles pulls a few tissues from her purse—"Get out of the way; let me do it!"—and kneels down in the other's place, unfolding the tissues and arranging them around the flaccid penis before starting to suck with a vengeance. After a few minutes laboring unsuccessfully on the recalcitrant piece of flesh, she's replaced by the first girl again, who launches herself at Ben's balls. During all of this, the object of their efforts keeps his eyes shut, pressing my hand to his cheek, repeating mechanically: "I want to stay with you. I want to stay with you." I push him away gently and say: "Go ahead. Go with them. I'll wait for you."

"Swear?"

"I swear."

Ten minutes later, he's back. Unbuttoned white shirt, white underpants. Smile.

"Now will you please dance for me?"

10

S o you managed to pull it together enough to work, after the party on Sunday?"

Lipstick in hand, Fleur is chatting with Poppy. They're sitting side by side in front of the big mirror in the dressing room. I blow their reflections a kiss as I enter the room and head for my locker. They keep talking:

"Yeah, I came in; I wasn't tired. I didn't drink that much at your friend's house. I can even remember what happened!"

"I can't!"

"Truth or Dare! You really can't remember? That young blond guy was a good kisser."

"I thought I'd been kissing someone, but I don't remember who!"

"The lawyer licked your right ass-cheek!"

"There was a lawyer there? Good thing we left at nine! Otherwise, who knows how we might have ended up!"

"Well, not in some big orgy. I wouldn't go that far . . ."

"No, but one or two little blow-jobs . . ."

While Fleur and Poppy were playing Truth or Dare, I'd been coming home from Ben's apartment. I didn't dance for him. The two girls hadn't been able to understand why I refused. "He's going to pay you so much money!" they'd squealed in my ear after dragging me into one of the bathrooms on the pretext of touching up our makeup. I'd thanked Ben for his hospitality and left. I didn't sleep well after that, and fatigue is setting in now. It seems like I can still feel last night's dancing thrumming inside me. It was hard to stand when I woke up this morning. Pins and needles in my thighs, knees popping, shins cramping. The first steps I took out of bed were a reminder of the sometimes graceful, sometimes obscene, frequently uncomfortable positions I have to contort my body into to be desirable, to make men horny. Male desire is a heavy burden to carry. Six nights a week (vacations are great for working) I'm an arching, swaying body, sinking into a full split to wow the audience. But the fatigue is getting more intense, feeding my doubt and my guilty conscience. When you're tired, you're vulnerable, and the guilt comes back full-strength. I have to stop doing this. But tonight I go upstairs again with Fleur and Poppy as if this life were mine. We sit down at a table without being asked. They're young, and there are three of them, three of us. But the conversation just doesn't flow, going in awkward circles. Irritated, Fleur whispers in my ear: "It's too early, they're not giving anything up. They need a few more drinks, the assholes." Then she says to the three men: "So can we all have a drink, or what? You ever heard of chivalry?"

Apologizing, they offer us some vodka and Red Bull and make more of an effort to engage us in conversation.

"So, did you spend Christmas with your family?"

Now Poppy is getting impatient. "We don't have a family."

"Oh—you don't?"

"No, we don't. Our mom's dead, and our dad raped us when we were little. So what? Why are you looking at me like that? It's the reason we're here!"

"Do you have any kids?"

"No, we're all menopausal."

We laugh and try to change the subject. Just then, the guy sitting next to me decides to talk.

"I'm getting married soon."

Fleur pounces. "Well, I hope she's sucked your dick plenty, because that's all over now!"

"It'll be fine."

Poppy takes over. "It'll be fine? Pfft! I've been here for years now, and not a single guy has ever said it was as good after marriage as it was before. Believe me, your sex life is dead."

I smile mechanically at Poppy's words, but I can't help thinking that she's probably right; that maybe he should travel instead of getting married so young, that maybe they all should, they should spend their time chasing skirts because it takes a lot of women to make a man. I get up and leave the table; the conversation is petering out again, and given how stingy they're being with the vodka, I don't think they're going to be spending much on dances, either. I head for the bar, scanning the clientele. It's only in a place like this that a woman can look every man she passes straight in the eye. I approach the one who doesn't avoid my gaze. He's chatty, so things are off to a good start. This is his first time in a strip club. I'm sure of it. I have a knack for recognizing people like me, the ones who are just getting acquainted with the world of the night. With me they're not as nervous; we're cut from the same cloth. The other girls are less reassuring for a novice. They've lost any sense of reserve.

He asks me for a dance; he wants to see what it's like. I love a customer's first time. It's my way of deflowering them, taking them to a place somewhere between childhood and adolescence for a moment of abandon, before they remember that they're men and feel all the powerlessness that goes with it. This guy looks to be somewhere in his early fifties, with locks of thick, graying hair that flop over his smiling face. He inspires trust. I can see the boy in his eyes. I can sense the animal in his hands. And I am slutty, sweet, crude, elegant. I am everything. I get inside him, gently. He has to lose his head. Yes, his head on a platter, mouth open, no more words coming out. Every woman that dances is Salome. That's why we dance, to watch heads fall, men vanquished. I examine his neck, caressing the fold of skin that would be the perfect place to bury my dagger. And slash! Decapitated. He closes his eyes and sits very still, back pressed to the bench seat. I enfold him tightly in my arms and offer him my breasts, stroking the nipple I know he's desperate to suckle, murmuring a few last words into his ear. He rummages in his pocket and hands me a twenty-euro note. I keep going for a few more minutes, just one more song, no more. Once again I'm a woman in love, a whore, an angel. He's already realized that after this, everything, absolutely everything he experiences, other women, their skin, their sex, their kisses—all of it will seem flawed. Nothing else will be as good, and that's why he'll come back again and again, seeking the sublimity and the muddled adulation of his own fantasy.

While I'm getting dressed, it's his turn to expose himself, talking about his life, his divorce, his difficult relationship with his son.

"That's why I came here tonight."

"What do you mean?"

"For my son. I wanted to give him an evening in this place; I've heard nothing but good things about it. Would you dance for him? I want to give that to him, for his eighteenth birthday."

"What a lovely gift from a dad! Yes, of course I'll dance for your son."

We go back upstairs together. He's in a hurry to go and find his boy; I'm proud to have been chosen to teach him this life lesson. Another head to cut off. I savor the delightful prospect of fresh meat. The DJ calls me over; it's my turn onstage. We'll meet up again right after my performance.

One spin, two spins, three spins. My head is whirling. I do the only pole-dance move I know, upside-down, clinging to the pole. When the world's upside-down like this I'm a kid again, too, playing on the jungle gym and the swing set, ready to fly, with that particular quivery feeling you only get from the fear of falling. And maybe it's because I'm a little bit drunk, my vision blurred by the lights, the dizziness, the darkness lurking everywhere, but I think—over there, on the opposite side of the room from where Rose Lee is dancing, talking to another dancer with his elbows on the bar—I see a young man I recognize. Him—here? I press my back to the pole as something inside me breaks apart. I sway in place, paralyzed with panic. I turn my head slightly—my customer is approaching the young man, pointing to the stage. This is worse than anything. A total catastrophe. A masterstroke of bad luck. I spot Iris passing near the platform. I call her over. "Please, please, take my place," I beg her. "I'll explain everything—just please, help me." I take my hair down to hide my face and flee to the dressing room, utterly terrified. I feel tiny and pathetic, teetering on my stilettos. Like something dirty. I want to disappear. To leave. *It's okay, it's okay, it's okay,* I repeat frantically in my head. *You got off the stage in time, he didn't see you.* But *did* he see me? Did he see me? I gulp some water. I feel as if I've run for miles. My heart is hammering in my chest. It's worse than that out-of-control feeling desire gives you. Why, *why* did I come in tonight? I was tired, exhausted, but it was the goddamned desire for money. That's what it was. The desire for money, and the physical excitement I feel when I do what I do here. Vanity. Nothing but vanity.

Iris, having filled in for me, comes down to the dressing room. "Rose, are you okay? What's the matter?"

"A guy I know . . . I don't know if he saw me . . ."

"You can take off if you want, you know. Tell me where you saw him, and I'll check for you. He might have left. I'll talk to Andrea."

I didn't know that, in cases like this, Andrea will let us look at the security cameras to see if a client we don't want to recognize us is still on the premises. It could happen to any of us. I check the cameras. They don't miss a thing. Eyes that see absolutely everything. I spot them, father and son, wandering through the main room, around the platforms, like they're looking for someone. Looking for me. Panic rips through me. I feel like my insides are on fire.

"Iris, here, look, please—it's those two, you see them? Do me another favor, please? It's just playing another role; it's good practice for you, right? Go and talk to them, tell them Rose Lee's busy with an important customer, say I'll be busy all night. And tell them I'm sorry, and as an apology I'm sending you to be the boy's birthday present instead. Give him a dance and try to talk to him—see if you can tell whether he knows who Rose Lee is. Please?"

She sets off on her mission. With Andrea's permission, I stay where I am, watching the security screens. Iris is skilled and smiling. I watch her head for the private rooms with the boy. Beneath the camera's watchful eye, she puts on the full show. I know her dance moves, her poses, all her ways of making the customer abandon himself. In just a few minutes she deploys her whole bag of tricks, interspersing erotic poses with resounding spankings. She's doing her job perfectly, but the boy sits perfectly still in the face of the onslaught. When she's finished dancing and is putting her clothes back on, he leaves without a word. Iris lifts her shoulders toward the camera in a shrug. I stay in the office until the father and son have left the club after making the rounds of the main room again, eyes glued to the stage.

"I don't know who this kid is, but he's impossible to talk to. I gave him a hard-on; that's all I can tell you."

I thank Iris. All I want is to get the hell out of here. The night is endless agony, struggling to quash my terror. *It's-okay-it's-okay-it's-okay.* Soon everything will go back to normal. I'll clean up the mess of my own desires. Rose Lee was just a detour, a digression. We're all entitled to a little detour, aren't we?

I'm not going to get a lot of sleep tonight. Just a few meters away from the stage where I was dancing nude, confused or enchanted or maybe filled with animal desire, was eighteen-year-old—what's his name again? Kevin? Bryan? A student in his final year, studying IT and business administration, who's often late for his classes, whom I frequently see running past my classroom door. Sometimes he hangs out in the corridor at the end of the day, talking with Hadrien and a few others from my class.

Tonight, he was almost my customer.

I have to stop doing this.

11

Piled untidily on my desk, a pile of papers calls out to me desperately. I never should have forgotten the students, my real work. Only a few days and twenty essays to correct separate me from the first day back at school. For just a few more nights, I will be the venal woman who wantonly turns her own body into a marketable commodity. I've asked Andrea to space out my work nights, but she begged me to come in every day until vacation ends because she doesn't have enough dancers. I wanted to cancel, to say I was sick. It would have been partly true, at least. Since I saw that student at the club, my migraines have started up again, and the insomnia, and the stomachaches. Whenever I'm at work, I can't stop staring at the door every time it opens—dozens and dozens of times. Rose Lee is slipping away from me, and the nights are becoming less profitable. I've started clearing out my locker. Last time, I brought home my shower gel and razors and perfume samples. Tomorrow I'll pack up the dresses I don't wear anymore. In the end I'll sneak out like a thief, because I don't have the courage to tell them I'm quitting.

I attack the papers with renewed dedication: assessment matrix, strict grading, symbol key for marginal notes. Ten, fifteen minutes spent on each one, no more. These aren't essays; the students aren't capable of engaging in true philosophical reflection yet—they're just exercises intended to help them gain some skill. Using the concept of responsibility as a starting point, they have to give one or more definitions, explore different lines of thought, possible problematics. These are the vital building blocks, not only of writing an essay, but even simply of developing a reflection. It takes work, for me, too. As I make my way through pages blackened by their efforts, with traces of folding and refolding at the corners and inky spots covered with White-Out, and their rough prose, struggling to put thoughts into words, I find myself touched by the imperfections. It's from all this, from their wobbly and tentative words, that I'm duty-bound to construct a coherent whole. On a separate sheet, I write down all the good things I find, however scattered or confused, in each paper. The answer key I'm going to give them will consist solely of their voices, the sum of their intuitions. I want each one of them to feel like they've touched on some truth. Wallen didn't grasp the legal implications of the concept of responsibility, but that's okay. She did make the connection between responsibility and freedom. Lény figured out the two meanings of the concept by researching the Latin etymology: *respondere* means *answer*. This helps us to define responsibility first as the ability to exercise good judgment and, second, as a burden we take on. Hadrien focused on the reflexive nature of responsibility: being responsible is to take responsibility. Some other students also managed to reflect on the internalization of authority, or the difficulty of knowing what we're really responsible for, because if we're supposed to postulate a link between man and his actions, like the one between cause and effect, how can we know how much of ourselves is present in what we cause to happen? What I'll need to explain to them next is that the idea of responsibility requires us to posit the premise of personal identity as: "I am the same." For how can a subject be responsible for all of its actions if it lacks substantive permanence? So, I am the same now as I was then. I am the same.

Three hours to mark twelve papers. I've done some good work today, only eight left. I draft a conclusion while considering what to wear tonight.

12

I go down to the dressing room to put on my mask and summon up some passion for the job. A swipe of blush on the cheeks, another line of kohl to darken the eye, a fresh layer of under-eye concealer, perfume, quick brush of the hair. The newest recruit sits next to me, blonde and creamy-skinned and looking like she's still in her teens, a pretty, well-brought-up doll with nothing slutty about her at all. Stage name: Rebecca. She's never danced in a club before, it's obvious. Later, on a quick pee break, I surprise her in floods of tears. She covers her face with her perfectly manicured hands.

"I wanted to do this because it was a dream," she says, "to be *that* woman, to understand how the night works, but I don't feel right, it isn't working, I'm not making any money, the customers are judging me—'What are *you* doing here? Why are you doing this? This isn't for you. You shouldn't be here. You're a good girl, I can tell. I do respect you, but honestly, I pity you girls. Why get naked just for money? It must be a hard, hard thing, I think, a really hard thing for girls to show their bodies like that. It's a shame, it's such a shame!'"

She dries her tears and redoes her makeup while Poppy hands her a shot glass and takes a half-empty bottle of Zacapa rum out of her locker. We each throw back a shot, one by one. Poppy glances at her breasts in the mirror and says:

"Strippers are crazy sensitive, all of us."

Back upstairs in the main room I notice a man staring at me, waving a ticket. He's sitting at a big table with a bunch of other guys, some of them younger, and a blonde girl in glasses who keeps gasping with excitement. Another girl, this one a brunette, is sitting silently next to the man, arms crossed over her modest cleavage. The man who motioned me over asks me to dance for the guy on the brunette's right. I come close, part his legs. The brunette grabs his hand and says, forcefully: "You can't dance for him, he's married. I'm his wife." I explain to her that it's just a present, that nothing will happen, it's just a performance. She doesn't back down, gets more aggressive, cursing in my direction. Conciliatory words rain down on her from the rest of the table: "Come on, it's no big deal, it's his birthday; you were okay with coming here, don't be jealous, it's his birthday present." She subsides but doesn't let go of her husband's hand. I don't look at her again, just do my job the best I can with her there, staring at me, and her husband grinning next to her like an idiot. This man who is hers—that's what she must be repeating in her head over and over right now, *He's my man! He's my man!*—this man gets visibly hard for my ass when I rub it against the front of his trousers, my spread legs, the voluptuous glory of my breasts just within reach of his tongue. With a quick movement, he adjusts his erect penis inside his underpants with his free hand. It's not just the man that his wife's clutching hand is trying to hold back. Poor woman. You can't keep a man from getting hard for a woman. That has nothing to do with love, or feelings. The body is our strongest reason for existing. I had to come here, to be Rose Lee, to accept the delicious exaltation of rubbing myself against thousands of hard cocks, the unvarnished confessions of so many men, to see the animal inside them and inside me, to stop resisting it. My mother was right: there are no princes or princesses. Suddenly, a heavy blow lands on my back. It's the outraged wife, hitting me, and her cries of "Stop, stop, stop it, you slut!" that force me to stop dancing. She's gone crazy, lost all control of herself, unable to do anything but shriek. Cries of "You're a whore, get away, you slut!" thud against me, and it hurts. I pick up my dress, and, without even putting it back on, I retreat. I flee to the dressing room and have a banana and, with Poppy's permission, a nip of Zacapa.

Every woman, young and old, beautiful and less beautiful, should do this job. For one evening, or a month, or for their whole lives. They would really see men, know what they're made of; it might spare them a lot of suffering.

Coming up from the dressing room I see her, on a sofa at the end of the corridor, away from the stage lights: the woman who hit me and called me a whore, crying. I pass her without looking at her. Her tears won't accomplish anything. I wish I could explain it to her, and that she'd understand. But I'm not here to be a psychotherapist.

Later, a man, reeling and stumbling, asks me for a dance. There are only a few songs left before closing time. "This is the last one," I tell him, "is that okay?" Faced with the prospect of the last dance, and the end of the night, he rifles through his wallet, pulls out his bank card, says, "I hope it isn't blocked." Who cares about an overdraft? The last pleasure of the night has no price.

Dreamless night. Not much money.

I head for the dressing rooms again. A small group of girls is clustered around a laptop, giggling. When I see what they're looking at, I want to laugh, too: photos of a micro-penis. They're heaping scorn on all guys.

The laughter is bitter.

In a few days, this will all be over.

I stuff all the dresses from my locker into my bag.

13

Papers graded and neatly stowed in the blue folder with my notes for the next class: two hours to discuss responsibility. Plato and Kant lie dissected on my desk. The bite-size morsels of philosophy I've chosen are the last thoughts in my mind to be inevitably scattered by my arrival at the club. The night has already begun at Dreams, and it's begun without me. Just a handful more hours, and I'll be finished with it. My agitation rises with each step. My impatience, too. What could possibly happen after this? What will be left in life to experience? I can feel, in every cell of my body, the brazen, furious vitality of someone standing face-to-face with a destiny they have chosen themselves, deliberately fulfilled. And, in the end, abandoned. That was the problematic of the student's papers: how much of ourselves is there in the things we cause to happen? How responsible are we for them? At the heart of that question lies the surreal end point of my journey: the dressing rooms and Rose Lee's locker. I just passed Rebecca on the stairs. She hasn't quit, then. Here, you come right up against the daunting prospect of being your own source of courage. Poppy is in the middle of changing her outfit. "Maybe it'll give me some motivation to work," she says, a hint of irony in her voice. Iris is huddled against the wall next to the shower, talking on the phone. She hasn't even seen me. I look around for Fleur. Her locker is padlocked shut, which means she isn't working this evening. Her absence is a relief. It'll make me feel a little bit less like I've lied. It's easier to disappear without a word.

I don't need much time to get ready tonight. Less makeup, no extensions. My hair looks fine this way, just natural. Tonight, Jo's the one going onstage.

I look at all the men fidgeting, drinks in hand, ties undone, smiling crookedly. This is it, the final act of the grand piece of theater I've allowed myself to indulge in. A lot of businessmen frequent this kind of club. They often come with their clients or future colleagues, pay for their dances, ply them with champagne. In the intimate atmosphere of the private rooms, negotiations are conducted and agreements reached, all parties pleased to enter into a contract that includes, between its lines, the big breasts of one, the naughty tattoos of the other, and all our smiles crowned with that intense scarlet that celebrates their glamour. The striptease artist drives the economy; she is its secret booster. I have the bitter impression of having contributed much more to the world's inner workings here than I have at school. Such is life.

Still. It's hard tonight without Fleur. I keep feeling tiny, nagging prickles of shame. Without alcohol, I forget to play the tease; I'm articulate, and men find themselves respecting me. This means they don't want to see me naked, and they don't buy tickets. The place is almost empty, as one might expect the night after New Year's Eve. That reassures me. If I luck out and get one good client, I can still have a good night. Otherwise, I'll just wait patiently for the end, giggling with the girls. I don't feel like trying to drum up business, and that's not my specialty, anyway. I go back onstage after a pee break. I sway my hips exaggeratedly; that's the least you can do when you're a stripper. A few moves later—really skanky moves—I stop short. Thomas is sitting alone at the bar. I launch myself in his direction. He looks at me and drains his glass. He's sitting up straight, perfectly sober. "You're not going to let me go home all alone tonight, are you?" he asks.

"I don't know. I could walk you to your door."

"My place doesn't have a sidewalk, or a door."

At five-thirty in the morning, I'm finally free. Rose Lee doesn't exist anymore, but I'm leaving with Thomas, because I want to. The embankment is swallowed up in darkness. Behind us, the Place de la Concorde and the glittering city. The Seine flows silently on our right. Thomas tells me some facts about the Champs-Élysées port and its fifty-one houseboats, which he calls "my neighbors."

"Mine's moored just in front of the Pont Alexandre-III. It's the biggest one. Belonged to my grandfather. Now it's mine, it's part of my heritage. I spent my childhood on the Seine. My grandpa and I used to walk to the Louvre. He took me to the museum every week."

"You must know all the collections by heart."

"Well, I know my memories of them by heart. And *The Wedding Feast at Cana*. Wait a second there; it's dangerous."

A light starts blinking. He holds out a hand to help me aboard. A row of potted bamboo plants forms a little hedge along the edge of the deck, concealing a wooden table and chairs. He offers me a seat and says he'll be right back, vanishing below deck and coming back up with a bottle, two glasses, and a blanket. The white wine he pours me melds with the icy night. I'm wearing a long white dress, and I must look like a firefly in the darkness.

"Just ten minutes, okay?"

I nod, incapable of refusing. He sits down across the table, facing me but not looking at me. Head tilted back, his gaze is fixed on the sky, even on this starless night. He starts to whistle, then hums a tune I think I recognize.

"'Casta Diva'?"

He continues serenading the sky, methodically, skillfully. I turn my glass, watching the wine dance. His phone rings, and he breaks off mid-treble. An irritated expression crosses his face as he looks at the screen, and he rejects the call.

"Come on, I'll give you a tour."

I gather up the blanket and the bottle. "Leave it," he says, "I'll do it," and holds out his hand again as we go down the stairs. His gaze falls on my stilettos, while mine drink in the sight of a black lacquered table, vases of white peonies, upholstered chairs, carpets, a stoup, Monet's *Impression, soleil levant*, a poster for the 1974 Centenary of Impressionism exhibition at the Grand Palais, floor-to-ceiling bookshelves filled with volumes, bottles and glasses, ornaments, framed family photos, chandeliers, magazines on a low table. The room is like one long stretch of light, with a grand piano at the far end, the final elegant touch in this glory of culture and richness. A slight, almost imperceptible sensation of floating completes the place's black-and-white perfection. Thomas glances at my shoes again.

"Should I take them off?"

"Oh no, never!" he says quickly. "A woman should never take off her heels. Can you play an instrument?"

"No. I took a class on musical theory and can recognize a treble clef, but that's as far as I got—with some music history and concerts thrown in, plus a fairly sensitive ear. I'm a philosopher, really. A philosophy teacher, I mean."

Thomas stops putting away magazines and says: "That's not possible; you're too well-dressed to be a teacher. Civil servants never have any style." Then, his back to me:

"The myth of the cave?"

"It's an allegory, not a myth. Plato, *The Republic*, book VII."

"Transcendental schematism?"

"Kant, *Critique of Pure Reason*."

"Monads?"

"Leibniz, *Discourse on Metaphysics*."

"Rhizome theory?"

"Deleuze and Guattari."

He turns and grins at me, his face filled with new excitement.

"Very unusual, mademoiselle! I tip my hat to you, and as a sign of my respect I'll start by playing a piece you might know, by Philip Glass. Please, come here."

I'm laughing, too, at finally having unmasked myself. It was nice to be Rose Lee, but it's not enough. For worldly, rich men, she's just another plaything.

He stops playing. "I really only like singing."

"Go ahead and sing, then. I'm all ears."

"It won't be perfect, and I hate imperfection. I don't like my voice very much."

"Still . . ."

He starts playing again, the notes merging with the words and silences that flow from him as he talks about his childhood:

"I used to dream of having a soprano voice; I wanted to be a woman, and to sing the way only women can. Kids believe in miracles. I ran away, looked for a doctor, a hospital, '*Operate on me, please, I don't want to grow up. I want to have a divine voice, a voice like an angel. I don't ever want to be a man . . .*'"

"Un bel dì vedremo" fills the room. He's Madame Butterfly now, all world-weary eyes and trembling mouth. *Un bel dì vedremo levarsi un fil di fumo sull'estremo confin del mare . . .*

I think I understand what he was looking at in the club, with that unseeing gaze, beyond the décor, the naked girls, the night, and his own drunkenness. The impossible life, the perfection of what doesn't exist. He stops singing like a woman now and says to me, "The high notes always used to make me cry with happiness. I wanted to be a castrato. Oh, well." He closes the Steinway. With a deliberately theatrical flourish, he presses his lips to the piano lid, brushing away an imaginary tear of adulation before putting down a little white pebble which he then crushes and grinds and spreads out with his credit card. Two white lines, perfectly parallel, equally thick, stretch away on the lacquered black surface. He takes a metal straw from his pocket—is it silver?—and holds it out to me. "No, thanks, I'm okay." He inhales one of the lines in a single sniff, looks at the other, and blows, as if to extinguish the candles on a birthday cake. The white powder vanishes in an aerial dance that is quickly swallowed up by the whiteness of the room: it's the same whiteness, but one lacks the purity of the other. Thomas picks up a remote control and aims it like an arrow at the ceiling. The strains of "Vissi d'arte" fill the room. He crouches next to me, caressing the heels of my stilettos, kissing the leather. One hand strokes upward toward my knee, then creeps higher. I take a step away.

I'm hot. I'm cold. I don't know anymore if I want to leave or stay, disarmed by this man who was—or wasn't—a child with an impossible dream. Is the story he just told me really his own? You don't joke around about childhood and its dreams. Should I laugh or cry? The thoughts are knocking around in my head. I can sense the wound, the cry, and they're tearing me apart. He gets up and offers me another drink. "You want one, right?" I don't say yes or no. His phone rings. He glances at it, and this time he answers. "Hello? Be quick, I'm with a philosopher. I mean it, man." He listens, doesn't speak, eyeing me the whole time. He hangs up.

"I'm invited to a party; it'll be going on for a while yet. You want to come with me?"

I force a smile. "No, thanks, it's already too late for me; I shouldn't even have come here." I scroll through my phone, looking for a number to call a taxi, but Thomas is quicker than me; he's hardly picked up his own phone again when the company's already on the line.

"Pont Alexandre-III, please, as soon as possible. Yes, we're in a hurry." He hangs up. "I'll drop you off," he says to me. "Just give me two minutes to change my shirt."

Coat shrugged on quickly, my purse under my arm, I wait. Two minutes is a long time when you're in someone else's house. A door closes, and then Thomas is there in front of me, completely naked. His face has the same expression I saw on him in the club, sprawled on the VIP couch, pouring a five hundred-euro bottle of champagne down his gullet. A sort of chaotic arousal propels him toward me; he wants to kiss me, to undress me. His dilated pupils are speaking, but it's the language of speed freaks, empty words, life rushing past in a pointless haze of chemically induced euphoria. His is a martyr's body, denied redemption, and I want to weep for him. It's a body that doesn't belong to anyone anymore, a body he's offering to me the way you'd give up your seat on a bus. I push him away and run for the dock.

There's a taxi waiting near the Pont Alexandre-III.

I go home.

PART THREE
ECCE FEMINA

Forehead pressed to the window, gazing out at the cars and the bus stops and the impatient pedestrians: the city waking up and beginning to toddle, as clumsily as a child. I, myself, am in the relaxed, loose-limbed pose of adolescence, because it's seven o'clock in the morning and I didn't sleep at all last night. In twelve stops, my life starts over again.

A half-smile flits across my makeupless face. There it is, still in the same place, the gray gate. It's like seeing an old friend again. I could almost jump for joy. Left foot, right foot, both feet together. *Jump, jump, jump high, Little Miss Grasshopper. Jump, jump, jump high, Little Mister Sparrow*. I'm almost there. Clinging tightly to the hope of a transfer, to all these men I love, Kant and the others, to my own good intentions. This world, disillusioned as it may be, is nonetheless reassuring. That's what I tell myself this morning as I make my way to the school.

The gate opens. For once, it isn't broken.

The students always come in earlier than usual on the first day back after a vacation. They cluster in noisy little groups, teasing each other, yelling, parading their triumphant insolence, sitting on the back of a bench passing a joint around. They're all there, acting like they rule the world. The boys, and that cruel age where you're nobody unless you have the right sneakers. The girls, and their too-short skirts even in winter, because that's what makes you a Free Woman. I glance at the crowd just once. That's enough to know he's there. And how could I not see him? Even from a distance, mingling with the others, even disguised, or blending into the dark night, I'd recognize him. He looks up, looks toward me, and stares at me with a man's eyes, which I can't see, but I can sense. My heart implodes. Straight as a steel blade, Hadrien watches me. Next to him is the student in his final year of IT and business admin studies. His name comes back to me abruptly now, with the cold-water-in-the-face slap of reality: it's Kevin. Martin had him in one of his classes last year. I pretend not to see them; it's too far, anyway, and too early, and maybe I'm imagining it. But my heart and my legs tremble, my briefcase almost falling from my hand.

Martin is already in the teachers' lounge. The universe is reconstituting itself in the vague smiles of colleagues, fingers and throats scorched by coffee and tea from the machine, stories about their holidays, glances at clocks or watches, open pigeonholes, cabinets closing, cold lunches in Tupperware containers on the table. I kiss Martin's cheek, pressing my lips to his clean-shaven skin, wondering if he can somehow sense all those mouths that wanted to touch me, the eager mouths of all the men who paid me money. Who knows if he, and all the other men in this room, can smell the sulfurous odor of my nights, the smell of money, of my exhilarating, intoxicating trade. Dirty money, they would say.

It's over.

Here, it's starting again.

In my pigeonhole, among the white sheets of paper, there is a red envelope.

Drancy, December 16, 2005

Dear Madame,

You get it. You've understood everything. None of the other teachers would ever be able to. You know just what to do, and suddenly I wish I had more hours of philosophy class. It's not just talk; you'll see, one day, how serious I am. I'm going to try to do well in your classes. I won't annoy you. I'll take notes.

I've been thinking about what Marcus Aurelius said. He's a good one, too. It helped me make a decision. I'm going to contact Anne. Nothing ventured, nothing gained. I know the fairy tales about the princess and her Prince Charming aren't real. I just want to be happy, and fulfill my desires when I get the chance.

It's helped me so much, writing to you.

Thank you.

Sincerely, your loyal student,

Hadrien

I'm early for the last hour of the day with my group of seniors. Even from the far end of the hall, I can make out Wallen in the dim light, standing near the door. As I get closer, I see that she's bent beneath the weight of her backpack, two plastic bags filled with chips and cookies and sodas at her feet.

"Are you done with class for the day, Wallen? Shouldn't you be there now?"

"Yes, Madame. I—I ditched, Madame."

"You ditched?!"

"Yes, sorry—but it's for a good reason, Madame!! It's Hadrien's birthday, you know. You gotta celebrate turning eighteen! And we all wanted to surprise him. We were counting on you. For the surprise, I mean. If we'd had your phone number, we'd have called you . . ."

"And my class? Isn't my class also important?"

"Yeah, but—"

"I've got your essays to hand back from before the break, too. And they were pretty good."

"Really, Madame? Oh, that's great—good news always comes in twos, that's what my aunt always says! But we can do both, can't we, Madame?"

So Hadrien's just turned eighteen. The coincidence makes my blood run cold. What if it had been Hadrien in the club instead of Kevin? He could have caught me in the act, too. I stare at the key in my hand. I fit it into the lock and turn it. Once, twice to the right. No, it must be to the left. It seems like it's just turning uselessly. The damn door won't open. I pull out the key and start over.

"Madame, are you okay?"

"Yes, Wallen, of course I am."

It staggers me that already I can't remember exactly, or maybe I remember all too well, the view from that stage that raised me above men, the world, everything. Truer than a movie, more beautiful than life, reality dissolving on contact with fantasy and with my happiness. *I wish I could tell you everything, too, my little Wallen; who knows what you would think—it might make you want to try it yourself . . . but me, I'm fucked.* That thought crashes through my mind now, too, because suddenly I remember the fatal sight. Kevin and his father. What did they see?

The door finally opens. I have to teach this class, to last fifty-five minutes without looking away from the students. I watch them arrive in small groups, with wings instead of feet— this is the last class of the day, their afternoon snack of philosophy, and we're going to munch on ideas. I arrange the seats a bit more whimsically, imagining a journey.

"You remember the peripatetic philosophers? Well, today we're going to have class Greek-style, with one extra little rule: to earn the right to feast at this banquet, you have to say something. Something intelligent and well thought-out. So, one good idea equals one good mouthful. Two good ideas, a swallow of Coke."

For once, everyone seems to approve. Good ideas always come along when you're focused on wanting something else. We're all ready to start the game, but the whole reason for this bout of educational theatrics is missing. Hadrien's not here. In a few more minutes he'll be late, and I'll have the right—but is it a duty?—to exclude him from participating in class if he doesn't show up with a note from the Student Affairs office. I look up at the clock like I'm praying to heaven. Tick. Tock. Tick. Tock. Tick. Tock. Eight minutes and fifty-two seconds late. He'll be here. Hope hums in me like a prayer. And time miraculously stops when Hadrien appears, frozen on the threshold, out of breath from running. He's hiding something behind his back. Everyone falls silent, a few students blocking the sight of the birthday treats, striking clownish poses.

"I'm sorry I'm late, Madame."

He comes toward me, his right hand behind his back, and I'm suddenly afraid. Reflexively, I take a step back, as if to sidestep the sudden exposure of my whorish life. But Hadrien, smiling, hands me a note from the Student Affairs office, justifying his late arrival. That was it, the weapon he was hiding? My first impulse is to grab him and hug him tightly, to run my fingers through his long, disheveled, darkly youthful hair and just talk to him. But I'm the teacher, so I ask him to sit down.

I go over my answer key on the theme of responsibility, the one I put together from all their words, while they stuff themselves, mouths full, cheeks rounded like children's, stifling a burp here and there (which I pretend not to hear) in the sleeve of a sweater, giggling convulsively. I launch into my explanations with a passion I'm not sure they've ever seen emanating from me. I'm floating, allowing the words to flow freely out of me:

"We have to question the nature of the link that binds us to our own actions, the internalization of authority, and through this, the reflexive nature of all responsibility. How much of ourselves is there in the things we cause to happen? What are we responsible for?"

Soon enough, the students tune me out; it's not worth trying to make them jump through hoops in the hope that they'll swallow some philosophy along with their Coke. Metaphysics can't hold a candle to chips and cookies. A fat lot of good I've done them today, just because I wanted them to like me, wanted to make myself feel better in my little job, to feel a little bit of excitement at returning to the normal life I'm reimposing on myself.

Only Hadrien tries to follow along, squinting to see the board clearly, raising a hand when all the others, backs turned, are busily making the last sweets disappear.

"I remember that personal responsibility is closely tied to freedom . . . but I don't really understand why. We're not that free."

"That's the whole problem. We're not that free."

Demoralized by my own lesson, I fall silent. I've just preached a mediocre sermon without meaning to, and the students were smart enough to ignore this sorry excuse for a Sunday school class. It's usually the reason they start ignoring me.

The bell rings.

Bye.

Everyone go home.

I stay for a few minutes to collect the empty packets, the bottles discarded on the floor beneath seats strewn with crumbs.

2

I'm waiting in the computer room for my turn at the photocopier. There are three of them, but only one is working today. That doesn't happen very often; usually we can count on at least two. The stress is palpable. One colleague has started chewing on little pieces of paper. Somebody else keeps having violent coughing fits. There's a clock on the wall just above the copier, staring down at the line stretching across the room like a worm. Will I make it, or not? A whole bunch of us have waited until the very last minute to prepare our lessons, or haven't prepared them at all. The machine heaves out copies breathlessly. I never know on a Monday what printouts I'll need for the week to come. After a few years on the job, you just stop lesson-planning at all. One two-hour class corresponds to up to six hours of planning. Upper-level teachers have between fifteen and eighteen hours of classes a week, not counting all the extra hours it takes to correct hundreds of papers. One essay, if read through and assessed correctly, takes between twenty and forty minutes. And then there's educational advising, team meetings, Board of Education meetings, core curriculum meetings, parent-teacher meetings, meeting-planning meetings, staff meetings. And the blank hours during which you have to be "available," and the hours you spend commuting, and the insomnia, and the hours emptied of any meaning or substance by anxiety and depression. School vacations are slow agony, but we quake in our boots at the prospect of going back to school. But we have job security, and people think well of us. The pay is crap, but a clear conscience and the illusion of being useful are priceless.

It's my turn. The machine begins spitting out copies of the quiz I've planned for today. I've laid out the concept of duty in a new way, in a table, to gauge their knowledge. The academic inspectors' orders are very clear: "Do not make things too hard for them." Obediently, I've made it as easy as I can: multiple-choice questions on philosophy, with three possible answers, and I'll be correcting the tests using green ink, because red is "traumatic." I'm not going to break my back over this anymore. I'm not being paid to philosophize, just to provide a sort of structured daycare. So be it.

"Who coined the phrase *Cogito ergo sum?* Plato, Cyrano, or Descartes? What does *Dasein* refer to? The Communist Manifesto of 1848, 'being there,' or 'the lack of being'?"

The photocopier makes an ominous noise, like a death rattle, but one that sounds almost like pleasure, too. Paper jam. I hold up my hands. "It wasn't me." Stifled little cries behind my back, general groaning. It's a true tragedy. Foreheads crease with anger. Eyes squint. The whole overarching failure of *homo technologicus*, summed up in a few sheets of paper mangled by a malfunctioning photocopier. We're all tied up in knots. But the worst is yet to come. I get lucky; after unclogging the machine, I've barely managed to finish making my copies when, on the touchscreen, the dreaded message appears: REPLACE TONER. I hightail it out of the room, leaving them to deal with the apocalypse. School is where you first learn to take delight in the suffering of others, and we've never really left the playground and its dirty games.

I feel around in my bag to make sure I haven't forgotten my letter for Hadrien.

Paris, January 10, 2006

Dear Hadrien,

I'm sorry for taking so long to write back to you. For reasons beyond my control, I couldn't read your letter until we got back to school. In the meantime, life may already have given you your answers. I don't know if you were able to reach your friend. Maybe the two of you are already back together.

I just have one small recommendation to make. Be careful, desire is a fickle thing. And sometimes, it has nothing to do with happiness. We all have to learn not to desire what's going to bring us suffering (read the Stoics), and we also have to learn to better understand our own desires (read Spinoza). Don't forget that a poorly understood desire is one that pushes us toward what seems to be good for us, but is bad in reality.

Good luck.

Sincerely,

Joséphine

adrien's only been showing up to my class about half the time for a few weeks now. I don't dare ask him for an explanation, much less jot a note in the log. There have been no more letters in my pigeonhole. Today he left after class without saying goodbye, head hunched. The uncertainty is killing me. Every night before I fall asleep, I relive the horror, the spectacle of my own pointless vanity: me on stage, and Kevin wandering around the room. I wake up every morning still with the same nightmarish images in my head.

In the teachers' lounge, it's almost the end of the day, gazes going bleary between the lines of papers being marked or straying toward the windows. The day is limping slowly toward the last bell. As I idly consider straightening up my pigeonhole before I go home, I glance out into the courtyard. The PE teacher is heading for the principal's office at a run. I can hear students shouting, but where are they? I shut the little door of my pigeonhole and, my things under my arm, I hurry out. Just as I reach the courtyard, I hear the PE teacher saying: "The area around the school falls under your purview, doesn't it, sir?"

"Yes," the principal replies. ". . . why?"

"Well, there's a dealer. The students told me he's selling hard drugs. Come and see for yourself so we can call in the police."

"But what am I supposed to do about it?"

"What? What are you supposed to do? I just told you! Look at the facts yourself, so we can act."

"But I don't see what—"

"Is the area immediately around the school your responsibility, or isn't it?"

I watch the principal recoil, his face flushing, and then head for the janitor's office. In a last feeble attempt at self-protection, he tosses a few words over his shoulder I wish I hadn't heard: "You know . . . that area, I mean . . . the actual boundaries are rather vague . . ."

"They're clear when it comes to students horsing around, but vague when it comes to drugs, is that it?"

Suddenly I see Hadrien striding toward the exit, with the measured, determined steps of a soldier. My colleague runs to catch him. I can see the anger in Hadrien's demeanor, the risk he's about to take, and I hurry, too, toward the school gate. I watch him as he keeps going, not looking back, grasping the metal fence and climbing it like a cat, disappearing with one final leap in the direction of the pavement, where I know he's about to unleash his fury. Hurtling through the gate just behind the PE teacher, I hardly have time to catch a glimpse of two bundles of muscle and sweat mixed with tears of rage tangled in ferocious combat before my colleague pulls them apart and the dealer flees. I have no words, just an outstretched hand to show my affection, because I wasn't wrong about Hadrien; I saw the depth of his emotions. The three of us walk back toward the school together, side by side, our silence broken only by Hadrien's words: "He's a criminal. He gave my little brother ecstasy. He waits outside the schools when they get out."

Hadrien could be punished for this. He left the school without authorization to fight in the street. I wonder what call the principal will make. I don't think I'll be able to look at myself in the mirror if I don't speak up. I barge through the door of his office without warning; he's putting on his coat, getting ready to leave. He puts on an expression of phony surprise and asks me if I'm all right—"You're pale; what's wrong?"—and then glances at his watch: "I don't have any time right now, I'm sorry. Please feel free to make an appointment."

I block the door.

"What are you going to do about Hadrien?"

"Hadrien? I'm not going to do anything because nothing's happened."

He puts a careful hand on my arm and moves me cautiously aside. "Please excuse me, Madame." He slips through the half-open door and is gone.

The next morning, Hadrien is loitering in the path leading from the bus stop to the school. I see him from a distance, and I know he's waiting for me. I feel my heart pound, the same way it used to when I went to friends' birthday parties in middle school and would stand there, not moving, not breathing, as if I were dead, waiting—in vain—for a boy to ask me to dance. Only once the party was over would I start breathing again. But you can't die from a dance you haven't danced. Close up, Hadrien's face is an exact map of his turbulent emotions. The fight with the dealer has left blue bruises on his cheeks and chin, and the dark circles under his eyes speak of a sleepless night, but the light in his eyes overrides everything else.

"Thank you, Madame."

"Nothing to thank me for," I tell him. "I didn't have to argue on your behalf. You won't be penalized."

"No, I don't mean for that. I don't care about being punished. You came out there with me to get rid of that dealer. That's the important thing."

I smile inwardly. I want so much to hug him, but I keep perfectly still.

He looks down at his feet, then adds:

"By the way, I'm reading Spinoza. It's really good, even if I don't understand it all. It's helping. Thanks, Madame."

Hands in his pockets, he tells me to have a nice day and walks away.

I got three calls from an unknown number during the night. One at 2:43 A.M., one at 4:12, and one at 5:58. I leap out of bed. I can't think about anything except who might have called me. That thought is enough to make the coffee taste less bitter; it's enough to make me put on a pair of five-centimeter heels and some sheer 20-denier black stockings. I slip my phone into my skirt pocket.

In the teachers' lounge, a few pairs of eyes lift at the sound of my footsteps. *Click-click-click.* Martin stops talking mid-sentence. I pretend not to notice. He's standing in front of Claire and Madame Louis, who are sitting next to each other and were clearly just listening to him. After a moment he goes on with what my arrival interrupted.

". . . there are a lot of egalitarian teachers who are all for streamlining the programs. There are two principles at work in their desire to dismantle schools as we know them . . ."

I slow down to listen.

"First, there's what I call 'hermeneutic castration.' I'll explain: students have become incapable of interpreting, unable to write essays or engage in discourse. In a world of entitlement, they're all about consumption; they're not about questioning, much less reflecting. They're incapable of stepping back, seeing things from a distance. They're all about immediateness, and, as we know, all culture—all thought itself—is really nothing but mediation. So the second principle is what I call the 'window principle.' Academic programs are just windows, but the mannequins are nude. We're selling subjects of study to the customers, but chronological order has been banned since the eighties; there's no substance anymore, only appearances, because we live in the moment now, and only in the moment. It all comes from bourgeois humanism."

I approach them and say only, "That's it. That's exactly it."

Young Claire's eyes glitter with tears. Madame Louis gets up and goes off to her job. So do I.

I string the hours of teaching together mechanically, without emotion. Not a quiver, not a qualm. I've promised myself. Because really, at the end of the day, it's just a matter of habit. One day I won't feel anything at all. No more disappointment, no humiliation, a non-life. I gather today's meager crop of homework, only around thirty papers for two classes, sixty-three students who know I don't have any real means of cracking down on them. We're basically forbidden from giving out zeroes, or even marks that are too low. I'm not even sure why I still bother giving them homework. What is there left for them to gain when there's nothing left to lose?

Last hour of class. A few faint whistles reach my ears. They're used to seeing me in flat shoes. Today's five-centimeter heels give them an excuse to be inordinately excited, to joke around. Don't react. Pretend to be deaf, blind, dumb. *So* much more intelligent than them. I'm laboring for their own good; I won't be distracted. I'm the one playing the lead in this movie. I'm an actress. And what a magnificent scene this is: life in a high school! That's what my instructor in the teacher training program used to say, back in the days when my naivete stood in for hope. I look for Hadrien's face. He isn't there. I keep moving and speaking, robotically. What a waste existence is, when you're just waiting for it to be over with. I take out my notes and read aloud: "Moral consciousness arises from an ambivalence of feeling, where a prohibition leads to the concealment of a desire . . ."

Lény, arms folded, is fidgeting in his seat. Wallen's not taking notes, doesn't even have a pen and paper out on her desk.
Their indifference is demoralizing.

"I'd rather just listen, Madame," Wallen says. "I can't con-
centrate if I'm writing."

She snickers. She thinks I'm a skank. At the same time,
Lény reels off a non-exhaustive list of their rights as students,
which includes not being required to take notes, because lib-
erty is sacred in France.

A vibration in my pocket drowns out the echoes of their
voices. The classroom ceases to exist. I pull out my phone. It's
that same unknown number. "Hello?" Silence. "Hello?" A
quivering, faint, faraway voice. I listen, ear straining, mind
frozen.

Back in the room, it suddenly occurs to me to ask for their
homework assignments. A pencil case lands next to my desk.
Silence. Eyes flit around the room in search of an escape route:
up at the ceiling, out the window, under desks, in backpacks. I
don't even try to find out who threw it. I walk toward them
and ask for their papers. Eight students out of thirty-three have
done the assignment. I caress the few sacrosanct pages handed
over discreetly by those who actually took the trouble to do the
homework, and slide them into an envelope. So that makes
about thirty-eight papers for ninety-six students. The incalcu-
lable failure—is it mine, or the whole education system's? Or
France's? Or all teachers? Or the Education Minister's, or his
wife's?—stretches out endlessly before my eyes, which settle
on the white stain of the dry erase board, a uniform blankness,
emptiness. I preferred the blackness of the chalkboard, the
squeak of the chalk. Now, turning my back to the class, I bid
my farewells to that white expanse. Every cell in my body is
aware of the enormous gravity of this moment, of this ending
of an era, of my life, maybe, and I give a helpless, crazy laugh—
so crazy that I gather my few things from the desk—pencil

case, bag, pen—and without so much as a single glance in the students' direction, I head for the door, which I open and then shut behind me, closing it firmly but not slamming it; that's better. A stage exit shouldn't be sensational, just so long as it's memorable, original. There it is; there's the scene my instructor was talking about. Quitting with panache. Or dying in the attempt.

The only sound in the deserted corridor, with half an hour to go before the last bell, is the light clicking of my heels. Behind me, I hear a door open and Wallen's voice, calling after me:

"Madame, where are you going? Class isn't over yet."

5

I'm dressed in white. I've put on a mid-season dress, even though it's a little too cool outside still. I've bought a bouquet of tulips and some women's magazines. She likes flowers and photoshopped models. I came early, to prepare myself for this encounter. We haven't seen each other in three months. It feels like forever. Fleur and the world of the night seem so far away now. I wonder if she's gotten a different haircut, or maybe some new highlights. I rule out the possibility of a boob job.

After checking in at reception I sit down in the waiting room. I stay still so my dress won't wrinkle. Everything around me is white, except the chairs, which are jade green, set out in rows. There's a copy of Monet's *Water Lilies* on the wall across from me. The air smells like disinfectant and medication. I bury my nose in glossy magazine pages. Their perfumed smell does me good. I look up at the sound of muffled footsteps coming toward me. A nurse says, "She's waking up, you can go in now. Room 203, end of the hall, on the left." There's no need for her to say anything else; she just smiles. She's seen hundreds, thousands of women in the same situation. That's her job: to listen to the cry, to read the anguish of that inner tearing that will bleed for the rest of their lives. I thank her wordlessly and stand up.

Fleur opens her eyes just as I open the door to her room. She smiles weakly, lying still in her drugged-up lethargy. Her hair is shorter and curlier than I remember. The violet shadows under her eyes stand out against the whiteness of her skin. Her pupils quiver with emotion. With pain. Fleur, a china doll in a white bed, groggy from the anesthesia, lifts her right arm and tries to interlace her fingers through my own. I gather her into my arms and kiss her hot cheek. My baby doll.

We're waiting for the doctor to come by and sign off, and then I'll take her home. I don't want to know why she made this decision. Suddenly I regret not having called her, gone to see her. The shock of being unmasked numbed my heart, erased at a single stroke all the new emotions that the night had brought me. Forgetting, that was what counted. But Fleur didn't forget me. Close your eyes and rest, baby doll. I'm here, and I'm not going anywhere. So beautiful, so vulnerable, she rests a hand on her belly, caresses it, then slaps it feebly. I open my mouth, but the words stick in my throat. Fleur presses a kiss into the palm of my hand. "It's okay," she says, "by tomorrow I'll have forgotten already. I should have been more careful. It'll never happen again."

6

L ying together in Fleur's four-poster bed, I hold Fleur while she methodically describes the nights, everything I've missed since I left. Holding hands, my body pressed against hers, I remember. The curtains and the soft lights, the erect cocks straining beneath trouser-fronts, the garter tucked full of tickets, the money, and Fleur's body. I know the creases around her knee, her nipples, her face, beautified with makeup or drawn with fatigue. I know the glitter of her perfection, the little flaw she hides with foundation, the shape of each drop of sweat. Her body, as if it were my own, which I clutch firmly against me under the duvet. I'm exhausted, but I can't sleep. Fleur has unleashed a tidal wave in my head, the urgent need to dispel the fear, maybe.

"I hung on to your locker. I figured you just needed some time, or maybe you had too much work. I mean, you're not going to be a civil servant your whole life, are you? You'll turn all ugly and badly dressed! I can just imagine you in ruffled old-lady dresses!"

Fleur eventually dozes off, and so do I. I have a dream in which I'm walking *en pointe* like a ballerina. I execute one pirouette, two, three. I'm wearing a pleated skirt and a black corset. My toenails are painted a gorgeous shade of red, and I'm holding the bottle of no. 11 Spicy Red nail polish in my hand. I'm looking for the road to get to school, but someone's shouting. Calling for Rose Lee. Whose voice it? I look left and right. No one is there, but I hear someone say: "I recognized you from your style. I hadn't forgotten you, Rose Lee."

It's six in the morning. I slip out of bed to make a quick stop at home before heading to the school. I don't take a shower or change my clothes. I want to hang on to our mingled scents, the remains of my makeup from the night before, my tangled thoughts. But without frills.

In the esplanade in front of the school, all I can see are enormous heaps of soot and garbage cans deformed by fire. I'd completely forgotten that the *banlieue* has been on fire for two days. Now it suddenly comes back to me. I wonder if I actually needed to come in today. What day is it? Spending time with Fleur has made me completely lose touch with reality. I pick my way across the debris. Inside the building, it's total pandemonium, people yelling. The teachers' lounge is like a town square on market day: the fishmonger and the baker trying to out-bellow one another, people milling and crowding and jostling. You can't hear the bell ring, and I have no idea whether there will be classes or not. The classrooms and corridors are just as chaotic. Students arrive in waves and leave just as quickly. Groups are forming in front of the school, shouting about the new labor laws the government's just introduced, protesting first employment contracts, which state that teachers under age 26 can be fired without justification after two years in a position, and clamoring in support of permanent contracts and their promise of job security (very expensive for schools). We're the ones who'll have to deal with the kind of outbursts and abuses that go along with this sort of protest, though. I bump into Hurley. "No class today," he says. "Everyone's coming out to join the demonstrations." He asks me to come along with him. "We have to keep an eye on the students, make sure they're safe," he says, beseechingly. He's scared. I'm sure his son, who's in his final year at another high school, is participating in the protests. In my colleague's awkward rush, I see the father desperate to find his little boy. I hate demonstrations. I've never participated in anything like this. The possibility of urban violence has always kept me far, far away from this kind of experience. There's no way I'm going out to scream about my anger and my rights and my misery in streets full of people. I decide to take advantage of this whole thing to get caught up on my lesson-planning.

I dodge and weave down the corridor, students and teachers hurtling past me like blanks fired blindly from a gun, all wearing the same expression of anxiety mingled with excitement. Passionate desire has finally touched this place, which has suddenly become a home, something beloved. I spot the principal amid the hubbub. He's coming straight toward me. It's too late to change direction, to melt into the throng heading for the street, the outside world. He asks me to come with him, and we battle upstream toward the office. As he rifles quickly through the pile of mail on his desk, I cling to my little water bottle, swallowing the repugnance this red-faced little man arouses in me, dissolving my fear of a sermon in a mouthful of water. I glance down at his stubby little fingers, the miniscule wedding band squeezing his left ring finger, his hands shuffling and rustling and folding sheets of paper, his index finger wet with saliva. He doesn't look at me. It's like he's taking his time, and I can almost hear the rackety clamor of his garbled thoughts. His Certificate of Professional Aptitude in welding hangs on the yellow-green wall behind him; I knew he'd started his career as a teacher specializing in that subject. There are framed photos on his desk.

"Do you need to take a few days, Madame . . . to rest?"

No beating around the bush, then; we've gotten right to the crux of the matter. This isn't the time to buckle under the fear and the doubt, to wonder, "What does he know about me?" I react. The best defense is always to attack. I complain.

"Sir, every day I find myself more and more overwhelmed by the enormity of the task. We as teachers don't have the proper working conditions to do our jobs anymore."

"You're too idealistic. Just focus on doing what you're paid to do and not leaving your students before class is over."

"Yes."

"And, also . . ."

". . . yes?"

"Also, there are some crazy rumors going around about you."

"What kind of rumors?"

"They're stupid. And what's more, *highly* unlikely."

"Oh, well, if that's all. Could this be retaliation because of a bad grade?"

"That's possible."

He gets up and holds out his hand to shake mine. I bounce out into the corridor, relieved to be away from those lightless eyes. I have a sudden desire to shit my pants—but also to laugh, to scream, to roll around on the floor. Everything seems unlikely, like reality is dissolving. I don't believe it myself anymore. Was I really Rose Lee? Could Kevin have seen me and not believed his eyes?

I run into Hadrien. He's all sweaty, his messy hair falling into his face, but I know his blazing eyes, his fiery heart. I don't turn around. I keep my head low and my steps quick, almost running, until his "Madame!" rings out like a plea. I can hear him coming to catch up with me. He lopes up and stops in front of me.

"What are you doing, Madame? Aren't you coming?"

There is revolution in his voice, the seeds of the kind of noble exaltation that will make a man out of him. It's like he's rising up against me and my apathy. *That's right, Hadrien, I was going to go and work, like an ass, while the rest of you take to the streets, hoping to make this world a better place . . .*

"Madame, the school has chosen me as spokesperson. I'm going to make sure no damage is done, you know?"

His voice cracks. In his excitement, he doesn't notice it. Unable to find the right words, he takes my hand. I follow him. I'm eighteen years old. Hope floods through me. We're free. For the few dozen yards I run hand-in-hand with my student, I can feel the universe quivering, the silent unexpected strength smoldering in Hadrien's heart. I release his hand before we reach the yard where his classmates are waiting for him, I let him go ahead of me, but I'm still following him, not taking my eyes off of him. This will be my first demonstration, a holiday while the city burns. I spot Martin in the crowd, standing with a few other teachers. I go to them, to march with them against the first employment contract legislation. This is a serious moment, but I still feel like laughing, like dancing. I stick close to Martin, who is much more focused than I am. A muffled noise, louder than all the others, makes me look around. Behind me, in a group of parents, Kevin's father is walking, looking for his son.

Martin and I walk through the deserted streets to number 12a. Not a trace remains of today's unrest; it looks like young Claire's housewarming party will be peaceful and pleasant. And really, there would be no reason for it not to go well. Easter vacation is only a few days away; we're all in a good mood. Martin insisted that I come this evening. I hate recreating the teachers' lounge outside school. But tonight I agreed, in order to face my own fears. I've always found these kinds of parties deeply boring, and every time I expect them to peter out without either excitement or surprise. For whatever reason they usually end early, with the guests wanting to get home before dark, or dozing off, or rapidly getting drunk. Tonight I try to take an interest in poor little Claire again, already burnt out by the job but battling on with a valiant heart and an iron will. That's youth for you, and its illusions. I also have a long discussion with Madame Louis, who, in a fleeting moment of inebriation, invites me to address her using the informal *tu*. I don't even flirt with Martin, even though the prospect is my only hope of briefly forgetting about Kevin's father. When we were all marching with the kids today, the man who was my customer turned his gaze in my direction. Without thinking, seized with animalistic panic, I left Martin, claiming a sudden migraine, and fled as inconspicuously as possible, keeping my head down and a hand pressed to my forehead. For once, I wished I wore a veil. God forgive me. But before I'd fully escaped the crowd and its agitation, I turned around just once without hiding my unveiled, confused face. And the man, whose first name I can't remember, scanning the throng for Kevin, saw me again. A thousand questions flitted across his face, and then a frown, and then a smile. It was a staggering moment, because I wasn't afraid anymore. In fact, I felt a sudden, profound desire to be recognized.

Even now, I allow myself to be swept up in the sense of detachment the nights have come to arouse in me. I would love to catch a glimpse of anxiety or impatience on my colleagues' faces. Who among them has experienced mad love, physical ecstasy? Who among them has made love with more than a hundred men or women? Who among them has seen America, Asia, Tahiti? Who is brought to tears by the second movement of Ravel's *Piano Concerto in G major*? Who thinks of nothing but seeking out the extraordinary, the unattainable, the perfectly impossible perfection of existence?

I lean with the full weight of my body against the balcony railing, searching for support, for a new equilibrium, perhaps.

"What are you doing?"

I answer Martin's question with another question:

"Don't you ever think of just launching yourself into the void?"

My phone pings. It's a message from Fleur.

7

We drop our suitcases off in the little one-bedroom in Vieux-Port, and Fleur gives me just enough time to take off my sweater and tights and, bare legs pale beneath my cotton skirt, we go out. Our arms, chilly at first, loosen and relax. Fleur wraps an arm around my waist and draws me to her, pressing kisses to my neck, like a woman in love. I'm excited to be here beneath this blue and cloudless sky with her, bathed in sunlight so bright it makes us blink. We head for the Plage des Catalans. Fleur bought two tickets to Marseille and invited me for a few days' vacation. She's forgotten her tears now, obliterated her grief with lipstick and nail polish. Guerlain Intense Red.

At 8 P.M. we take a taxi to the 8th arrondissement. "You're going to love my friends," Fleur assures me. She's loaned me a dress, wants me to be extra pretty. The order to be beautiful amuses me. It's Givenchy, pure silk, with a plunging neckline. "I go to private sales," she says, as if justifying her possession of haute couture. "You'll have to come with me next time." I nod as we pull up at our destination, a house surrounded by cascades of light.

"Looks like we're the first ones here . . ." Fleur kisses the cheek of the man who's come out to greet us. "This is Joséphine. You used to have the same job."

"We did? Fleur didn't tell me," I say, surprised.

"I think she wanted it to be a surprise. I started my career as a teacher, yes. But all that's a long way behind me now. Except— well, come in. You'll see."

Marc, the owner of the house, ushers us into his living room, which is dominated by an impressive library of books. Shelves of mostly French literature stretch between the black leather armchair and the crystal-and-china-laid table.

"In choosing literature and teaching, I broke away from what you might call the family business," he explains. "But they pulled me back in soon enough. Like my father and my uncle, I became a nightclub manager. It's not literature, but the people are often very interesting, with life stories that deserve to be told. That's the most fascinating part of the job."

He pours us each a drink. I savor the champagne in little sips, to make the pleasure last. Along with Fleur's presence and the aftereffects of the sun, the bubbles dissolve the last of my remorse about going away. I'm entitled to a few days of relaxation; I'm allowed to forget all the work I was supposed to do over the Easter vacation, still waiting for me at home.

Marc gives me a tour of the house, shows me the garden, where a lit-up swimming pool reflects our images like a mirror. The doorbell rings, and he hurries off to welcome his guests. I stay there, breathing deeply the coolness of the evening, waiting for its sobering effect. But the voices coming from the living room sound familiar. I go back inside. Champagne glasses in hand, already comfortable in their light clothes, Poppy, Rebecca, and Mélisse—whom I know only by sight—are standing in the living room. There are two young men with them. The moment they see me, they turn from elegant queens into squealing little girls. Fleur jumps up and down and claps, pleased with her trick. So this was the surprise she had planned for me. They're here for three weeks, dancing at the place owned by Marc and his two partners, who are all friends with the owner of our club in Paris. I wonder if Fleur's going to try to convince me to start dancing again. It's out of the question, but I'm not angry with her. I feel good, being around them. It's not just the champagne, the marinated tuna, the filet of John

Dory with citrus and leek butter, the vanilla millefeuille. Nor is it the shelves of literature lording over our enjoyment, or the Givenchy dress. It's the indescribable rush of life, surging through me like a dizzy spell, the fantasy of freedom, the joy of knowing that it can all stop right here, before the dances, before the night. Fleur climbs up on the table, her bare feet deftly avoiding the plates and half-full glasses. We watch her strip with slow movements. Naturally sensual and erotic as only she can be, she offers us her breasts. She is sublime, bury-ing all sorrow beneath perfectly rhythmical movement. Fleur, who always wants to go further. I climb onto the table with her and dance her dance, holding her to me. No, Fleur, not your G-string. *You* are beautiful. Dance with me.

8

The next evening Fleur and I visit Marc's club. Near the catwalk are two little round stages, like carousels for dolls. Downstairs, there are elegant alcoves which, draped with curtains of transparent pearl beads, serve as private rooms. Fleur goes to get ready, and I follow her into a small room that's been transformed into a dressing room. The other girls are already there. It's only now that I notice Mélisse has a different haircut, that Poppy's wearing extensions, that Rebecca's got a new pair of tits. Adorned with her own nudity, she stands still in front of the mirror, gazing at herself appraisingly, and Fleur tells her distractedly that they look great. I stare at their muscled legs, excited fingers fluffing their hair and unhooking their bras and slipping off their panties and adjusting their G-strings. Their red lips and smoky dark eyelids. I try to imagine their first time on stage. Awkward young women, almost too nervous to move, sometimes tripping over their own feet, wondering, *What do I do? What does it mean for a woman to be sexy?* Now they know.

Leaving them to finish getting ready, I go upstairs and find a seat near the bar. Bit by bit, the place fills up, men leaning contentedly on the counter. Poppy is the first to dance. Her smile is dazzling, her face like a pretty doll's, her grace and elegance otherworldly. It's as if time stands still when she's on stage. Something inside me wants to call out, "Encore!" It worries me because I'm done with all that, and I have to remind myself of it.

Now Fleur makes her entrance into the main room, enveloped in a long, flowing, transparent dress. I feel just as male as the men around me, my eyes just as hungry, my desire to see her naked just as strong. She comes in my direction, but before she reaches the bar a customer stands and asks her to join him at his table. I don't like that hand grasping her forearm, that head bent toward her shoulder, that mouth already trying to kiss her neck. It makes her laugh. She pushes the man away delicately, moves the chair so she can sit across from him, legs crossed, one hand resting on her bosom. It's enough; he understands. She's thirsty. He takes a bottle of Dom Perignon from the ice bucket.

Her turn on the stage finished, Poppy comes to lean on the bar with me, turning occasionally to look at a man drinking whisky. I watch her negotiate a dance with him.

"You'll have a good time with me, you'll see."

"Yeah, but what are you gonna do that's better than the others? Tell me. Explain it to me."

"I'm an experienced woman. Trust me."

"No, that's not enough. I want details."

"Okay, look, this isn't some Marrakesh souk. I'm not selling carpets, get it? Take it or leave it. I don't give a fuck, okay? I've already bought my house with your money, all of you. Now get the hell away from me, asshole!"

Poppy turns back to me. "Come on," she says, "let's go down to the dressing room, I want to change. I don't like this dress."

Fleur's already in the middle of a private dance with her customer. I catch a glimpse of her as Poppy and I pass the alcoves, her body swaying and arching, pieces of her appearing and disappearing through the curtain of pearls.

She's still there when I emerge from the dressing room with Poppy. Her body fragmented, Fleur is light and shadow, naked, always naked, Fleur. I know this is going to last a while, that she's going to get a good night out of it.

I'm dead on my feet with exhaustion, but I wait until, more than two hours later, she comes to find me at the bar, where I've practically taken root in my chair. She wakes me up, her giggle childlike, tipsy on happiness and champagne bubbles. She shows me the night's earnings, proud, on the verge of crying, laughing at her own tears.

"Stripped him bare, did you?"

"Down to the skin, honey. He walked out of here like a plucked chicken. Tomorrow, you and I are going to have ourselves the biggest seafood feast ever; how does that sound?"

9

Tonight is my last night.

"You know I really do have to go, right? I have work to finish before school starts up again."

Fleur gets angry, then pleading, then threatening. Feigns incomprehension, because she knows that what I truly want more than anything is never to leave her again. "Stay," she insists. But I can't, I must not, even though the separation is wrenching. The days Fleur and the others have left here take on the aspect of a whole series of experiences I'm about to miss out on. What a waste, to catch my train, to deprive myself of them.

Fleur doesn't speak much. She spends the night drinking, taking on a string of customers, making cocks hard. She comes over to check in with me after each dance: "Guess how many private dances I've done tonight!" She forgets everything when she drinks. "Tomorrow I'll take you to Cassis," she says. No, Fleur, my train is tomorrow. You can go to Cassis with the others, maybe, but I've got to get back to Paris. She goes away annoyed, comes back fifteen minutes, half an hour later, asks me again, "Guess how many private dances I've done tonight! Tomorrow I'll take you to Cassis."

At closing time, I leave with Mélisse. Fleur has disappeared, gone off with a customer, maybe. I go to bed but can't sleep, which is just as well, because I hear Fleur when she gets home, finally. I don't ask her any questions. I know she never wants to stop, never wants to sleep, because "to sleep is to die," she says. She presses herself against me, kissing my hair, my eyes, my mouth, my hands.

The next morning, she comes with me to the station.

10

After Marseille my nights are peaceful. I sleep deeply, without nightmares. No tears when the alarm clock goes off, no diarrhea. The horizon is wide open. If the body is well, so is the mind. My sense of well-being is so palpable that I feel like I'm flying. I walk as if I were dancing.

This is the last back-to-school before the long summer vacation, the only time of the year when I don't want to barf up my whole life.

Not only do I *not* try to miss the bus, but I even leave early so I'll have time to savor this moment of happiness for more than eight thousand teachers in France. On our agendas, after the pages where we put an *X* for each day worked, after the months crossed out with a red pen, we only have to hang on for a few more weeks before the end of another school year. Every day is a last day, now.

A few stops before the school, Wallen, Lény, and some other students get on the bus. Usually when this happens I hide behind a novel or a notebook or a magazine, a hat pulled low on my head and a forbidding look on my face, telegraphing the message, *No one speak to me.* But today I look up at them, and receive a shower of "Hi, Madame!"s. A few passengers turn to look at these students, who always delight in being noticed, in making a point of their presence in the world. *We're here, and we exist, and we need you to know it.*

Wallen approaches me. "What're we doing today, Madame? Can we study? I mean, we're done with the syllabus, so . . ."

"No, we're not quite done with it yet. It's your responsibility to study on your own time, young lady."

Wallen looks crestfallen, but we've already reached our stop. I watch them jostling and tumbling off the bus, coming perilously close to knocking a frail old lady off her wobbly feet and almost taking one of the bus doors with them. Lény was holding one of the sliding doors when Wallen grabbed the sleeve of his faded jacket. The doors finally close after two or three clacking tries. But I haven't budged. Still firmly planted in my seat, I give them a little smile out the window, watching their shocked little faces, suddenly very childlike in their astonishment. I can almost hear the confused words swirling around in their minds: *What's she doing? Where is she going?* The bus pulls away, and they follow it with their eyes, standing motionless beneath the little shelter, suddenly lost. I want to wave to them, *Au revoir les enfants*. I just want to walk a bit, that's all. I get off the bus after two more stops. Coming back, I spot Wallen, still sitting in the shelter. She gets up when she sees me and runs toward the school entrance.

In class a few hours later, I'm handing out fact sheets to help the students study for their exams. Wallen almost literally jumps for joy.

"I knew you wouldn't just abandon us, Madame! I knew it!"

Hadrien has carefully organized all his class notes, the papers neatly stacked. I spot certain words underlined in green. He closes his binder as I approach. My heart leaps. I know he doesn't usually spend a lot of time on his notebooks. Hadrien drops his gaze and elbows Lény, who is wrapping adhesive tape around his fingers. It crinkles, and the class snickers. A paper plane lands on Lény's seat. It's one of the sheets I just handed out. It's started again, the exasperation, the inevitable migraine. I remember my teacher-training instructor's advice: *You can also pretend not to see or hear.*

Deafness, muteness, blindness—all strong points for becoming a good teacher. Well, my teaching authority may be all but non-existent, but I'm not deaf, or mute, or blind. The words come out involuntarily. I don't want to pretend anymore.

"I wouldn't crack up like that if I were you. Sitting there on those benches you've ruined with your filthy little carvings. You're shooting yourselves in the foot."

Wallen looks up and puts away her nail file. Lény, who's gotten to the end of the roll of adhesive tape, stops fidgeting in his chair. The hum of background noise grows softer. Hadrien takes a deep breath and lets out a long, forceful "Shhhhh!" His face darkening, he leans his elbows on his desk, fixing me with an uneasy, penetrating gaze.

"Everyone thinks you're idiots. The Board of Education, this institution, my colleagues. And everything's set up so you'll stay idiots. Haven't you wondered why they keep streamlining the curriculum? Doesn't that make you think? I'll tell you why it's happening. Because they want to give you less, and less and less, to make your parents, and the public out there, and the whole world think that you can adapt well and quickly. That you're all very intelligent. But in reality you're being dragged down, because they *need* you to be ignorant and unable to think in any deep or complex way. That's why you should be weeping and wailing and begging us on your knees every single day to teach you history, and literature, and grammar and syntax—begging us to give you whole books to read, to treat you like real students whom we *require* to be silent, take notes, have some discipline, and make an effort!"

For once, my voice is the only sound in this room, which is never silent except at night or during vacations, when the whole school is deserted. Maybe it's my emotion, the sudden uncontrollable impulse that has seized me, the overwhelming sense of powerlessness and frustration, all my pain as a teacher concentrated into this single outburst, but I think I see tears in

Hadrien's eyes, like something in him is breaking, or being reborn. I hear the silence of the others, their presence, their straining ears, their guilty faces. I see their dismay. Some of them look contemplative, eyes fixed on the notebooks they've taken out. Others sit up ramrod straight.

"Okay. You're going to read the study sheets I've put together for you. We'll go into more depth with them next time, so think of some questions. Take the time to reflect."

I end the class in silence. For the first time, the students put away their things quietly when the bell rings, and file out calmly. Thirty-three kids say, "Bye, Madame, thank you."

I'm drained. I head for the computer room. It's been weeks, if not months, since I checked my professional e-mail account. I hate doing it, too. Whenever I connect to I-Prof, I feel like I've suddenly lost the ability to read. I click on my inbox. I log out. I put the computer in sleep mode. My brain, too. The news of my transfer is so unfathomable that I don't believe it at all. There must be some mistake, that's the only explanation, a glitch in the computer system; they happen so much. I look in my pigeonhole, sure I'm going to have a letter from the ministry notifying me of the error.

11

He's waiting for me at the far end of the square, under the weeping willow, facing the Pont-Neuf. I slow my pace in my stilettos; I want to put my elegance on show for him. He's never seen me in high heels. Dressed in black, he's smoking a cigarette, his other hand clutching a copy of Descartes' *Metaphysical Meditations* to him. I smile, thinking of the first time Martin made me laugh, with an outrageous story about King Henri IV—nicknamed the Green Gallant for his womanizing—and male weakness. "I don't understand men who cheat," he often says. I find it funny.

He tosses away the cigarette and hands me the book.

"Fascinating stuff. Mind-boggling. But I prefer literature. I don't think I would have made a good philosopher. I find the pure concept aggressive. Powerful, certainly, but, at bottom, terrifying."

"I like the way you attribute souls to things that don't have them. You're right, though; the concept *is* terrifying."

I come closer, and arm in arm, we walk toward the outlet of the square. I offload the usual complaints.

"I'm just totally worn out; I can't even enjoy the end of the year anymore, because I know it's only going to start all over again. I feel like the world is crashing down, like my life's at a dead end. Another school year, coming for me like the Grim Reaper, and all I want is to get the hell out. I hardly slept last night. The thought of next September makes me feel sick, like I'm a lamb being led to the slaughter."

I want to tell him everything, confess my escape and the relief of it. The night, and all the rest. Sometimes I feel like he's always known.

"Yeah, me too. And the fact that in a few months we'll be back, hardly able to hold our heads up, with a whole new bag full of nightmares, a smiling hive of worker-bees of the mind. The worst part of it, Jo, is that, for way too long now, I haven't felt like we're on vacation even when we are. Work isn't work anymore, time off isn't time off; it's all blurred together. There's no more intellectual tension, and so it's not even a relief anymore when it ends. It's like the apocalypse; nobody wants to do this job anymore, it makes you ill. Depressed. And next year, our dear old principal—I've heard this from a reliable source—is going to find new hires by posting classified ads online. You must be really pleased, though, with your new gig . . ."

"You found out? I was going to tell you today!"

"News like that travels fast."

The e-mail I didn't dare to believe had turned out to be true. I called the Board of Education, and they confirmed it. I'm being transferred. The thing is, I don't have enough points for this particular transfer; that's why I was so skeptical. I'm being transferred to the Lycée Jean-de-la-Fontaine in the 16th arrondissement, Paris. What luxury. It's better than winning the lottery. Sometimes it's when you stop hoping for something that it happens.

Martin has reserved a table on the terrace at a place on the rue de Buci. Hopefully the red wine we order will pull me out of the state of inertia I've been in since the transfer news. I'd stopped believing it would ever happen, and now it's fallen into my lap. What am I going to do? I have to go, in any case. The State requires me to; I'm a civil servant. I've just been promoted. I'm going to be teaching *khâgne* and *hypokhâgne*, the advanced placement and university-level classes. I'll be among the elite, one of the grunt teachers transformed at last (because of the higher pay grade) into a respected civil servant, picked out through the process of so-called natural selection to teach the Holy Grail of educational programs, one in which the kids, those privileged kids, listen, take notes, do the work, and respect the teachers who are their transitional guides to certain success. Another glass, please. I'm such an ingrate, getting plastered, unworthy of so much good fortune. I should be over the moon, and I can't even bring myself to care. My thoughts swirl in a muddy haze of alcohol and new emotion. I imagine telling Fleur. Who knows what she's doing at this moment? She didn't answer my last text.

Martin's eyes are very bright, like mine. This is the first time I've ever seen him knocking back one glass of wine after another, drinking hurriedly, anxious to be carried away somewhere: doesn't matter where, just somewhere far away. At the same time, I can feel Rose Lee creeping in, into the hand I run through my hair, the legs I cross and squeeze together hard, as if to prevent the possible explosion. I have to hold her back, to stop this woman whose gaze can turn any man into a king. Martin thinks he hears the summons, strokes my hand, leans closer. I let him do it, but I don't react. He starts speaking then, as if the words might complement his actions, or maybe downplay them.

"When I think of what I heard about you—it's stupid. So stupid that I've never even wanted to mention it to you."

"About me? What do you mean?"

"It was months ago now. Time to move on, right? And anyway, it was just a flash in the pan, some student's idiocy that never went anywhere. Just pointless gossip."

I withdraw my hand from beneath his.

"Tell me."

"It's ridiculous, Jo!"

"Make me laugh, then."

"Okay, but I warned you, it's stupid. Kevin, who was in my class last year—he's friends with one of your students, and I more or less surprised them in the middle of a conversation, you know sometimes I like to play basketball with them—anyway, this Kevin thought he'd seen you in a strip club. You, a stripper! Can you imagine?"

"That's pretty crazy, yeah. What did the other one say? The other kid?"

"Oh, your student just laughed. I think I remember him saying you couldn't dance because of some big problem with your knee, or your back, I can't remember. Is that true, Jo? What's the matter?"

"Nothing, nothing. Is that all?"

"Think so, yeah. See, just bullshit. I told you. Obviously, I didn't take it the least bit seriously. You're too intelligent; you'd never do something like that. You're not the type to play that card; you aren't a . . . well, you know."

I'm offended by his way of thinking. So offended that, absorbed in my own concealed anger, I don't see him leaning toward my face. I barely avoid a kiss. "Forget it," I tell him simply. There's no flutter in my gut, my thoughts motionless in my head, a flat ECG.

12

M y greatest success of the year unfolds right before my eyes. Before the start of class, the students rise and stand up straight, unmoving and silent, waiting for permission to sit down. These past few weeks I've taught the lesson in a silence broken only by their questions. The students have filed up one by one at the end of each class to hand me the homework that didn't get done over the course of the year. I've taken on the additional workload happily. It's the grand finale of the fireworks show, the unhoped-for cap on a school year that ends today. The big day is here, but the thrill of it is muted. I'm relieved, but not happy. And yet I've always been delirious with joy on the last day of school, even more so as a teacher than I was as a student. Not today.

I never have an actual lesson during the last class of the year. We talk, we improvise a little party, we say nice things that erase the memory of the other, less nice things that have often marred our exchanges. Ten more minutes. I can't stop glancing at my watch. These last few moments aren't even the best part; that comes the next day, when the relief is so immense that you feel like an enormous weight has been lifted from your shoulders, like you're floating among the clouds, soaring in the great blue yonder. I've already stowed away the sheet of paper they filled with little notes and words of affection, like a goodbye letter, a trophy to be framed, to remind myself that all is not lost, that I'm a good teacher in the end. *Thank you, Madame, you've taught me to like thinking . . . Bye, Madame,*

I'll never forget you . . . I hope we'll see each other soon, I'd like to continue with philosophy, can I contact you for some advice? . . . Thank you, Madame, you've helped us, and that's priceless . . . Drawings of hearts. It's all so sweet, always touching when all they remember is the happy ending. I remind myself of that, too, so I don't descend into mawkish sentimentality, don't make the mistake of believing they really never will forget me. We promise to see each other, to organize a get-together, maybe lunch, after exams. The students say it every year. And then they forget.

I slip out after having wished them the usual things, happiness, success, good health. I look one last time at Hadrien. I'm forcing myself to pretend he's just another student. That's what's hard to swallow.

Back in the teachers' lounge, I empty my pigeonhole. There's a note from the janitor asking me to stop by and see him. Before I do, I send Fleur a quick text. After the trip to Marseille, she went to Miami with Rebecca to dance in some trendy club. I've gotten a few photos of the two of them in bathing suits, always very sexy, lying on the beach, smiling widely. Fleur loves going to the United States; it makes her feel like an outlaw—it's illegal to work there without a green card, but a lot of clubs look the other way. This kind of professional tourism is well known, it's why you can't travel with platform heels and stage outfits in your suitcase, or you risk being sent back before you even leave the airport. Fleur explained the whole thing to me with a certain pride, as if her trips were missions she'd had fun carrying out. I know she's worked in New York and San Francisco. She usually goes once a year, twice at most. She might even be back in France by now.

In his office, the janitor gives me a big hug and wishes me nothing but the best, says, "I'm so happy for you. The 16th arrondissement, it'll change your life." He hands me a little package. I slip it into my bag, keeping it to open on the bus.

Inside the red wrapping paper are a letter and a black four-hole punch. My snort of laughter makes the lady sitting next to me jump. I can admit, now, that I was hoping for one last letter from Hadrien, but I never expected him to give me a present. What floors me is the thoughtfulness of this young man. He remembered. It hadn't been a ploy to get his attention: I genuinely couldn't figure out how he'd punched that pattern of holes in his papers. I was only familiar with two-hole punches, which always result in a frustrating and hopeless struggle to make the holes in your paper line up with the rings in your binder. He hadn't laughed at my befuddlement, only assured me that four-hole punches did exist. He must have remembered the sorry state of my binders.

Drancy, June 8, 2006

Dear Madame,

This year was by far the best one I've ever had at school, and that's not because it was the last one. It's because of you. I'm writing to you one last time to say thank you, from the bottom of my heart, for everything. I didn't understand why we had to study philosophy, but I get it now. It'll stay with me for the rest of my life. I also asked you how it works. Living. I remember that. Do you remember? That was when you talked to me about Descartes, and, like him, you told me to study the great book of the world. I've reflected a lot about that great book of the world. But I've also read Spinoza, and I bought Seneca's On the Shortness of Life. *It excited me so much—philosophy, and experience, and the rest. All of it. And you, especially. I feel like I've learned a lot by watching you live. You've mentored me so well, because in your letters you showed me that philosophers' thoughts can help us understand life.*

I've been studying Spinoza really hard for the exams, and I learned this phrase by heart: "Do not mock, do not weep, do not wax indignant. Understand." That's what I've done with you. I know you were dancing nights—maybe you still are— but you're so different from the other teachers, and most of the adults I know, that it doesn't shock me. What an example of freedom. You amaze me. I've watched you a lot. You're very beautiful, Madame. I hope you will always be yourself.

Our paths are diverging, but please know that I'll always keep you in my heart.

Affectionately,

Hadrien

P.S. About Anne, by the way—we had a bumpy reunion, but we're good friends again now. Maybe something will happen.

Hadrien's letter makes me feel pain, and deep relief. Jo is saved; Rose Lee wasn't her demon. The other memory comes back to me: it was pouring rain that day, and when Hadrien asked me the question—"How does it work, living?"—I'd been tempted to answer with a trite "I don't know, nobody knows." But I loved this student, so profoundly different from the others, and so I owed him all my intellectual honesty. The injustice of love. I hadn't just talked about Descartes that day, the experience of life and of the self. I also said that living means wanting to live. It means acting. Acting as if. Like a game. Like the child who doesn't see the disparity between the world and its own senses. As if we aren't born to die. Were you ever a child, Hadrien?

I remember perfectly now.

"We aren't born to die." He repeated that phrase over and over, that day. "Living means acting as if we aren't born to die."

13

I walk the nocturnal streets, but I'm not simply wandering anymore. The Parisian summer night is a source of pleasure even in the aimlessness that has seized me with the end of this school year. Just as I hail a taxi, my phone rings. It's Poppy, crying on the other end of the line at three o'clock in the morning. I can't understand anything she's trying to say. I hear her say Fleur's name, and "Don't you know what happened? It's horrible, Rose . . . Rose, where are you?" My thoughts of the school year just past, and Hadrien, and his last letter are wiped from my mind at a single stroke. I ask the driver to take me to Dreams.

The lights are just like I remember, and the girls with their perfect bodies, but I don't recognize any of them. Where are my friends? I'm heading toward the dressing room just as Poppy comes out. She flings herself into my arms and sobs. Everything's happening too fast. Where is Andrea? Where are the others? And Fleur? Where is Fleur? Poppy's crying hard, but her words carry over the music, go beyond the night. Something in me stops living.

Fleur is dead.

Poppy is shaking, her eyes swollen from weeping. She gasps for breath.

Fleur is dead.

I push Poppy away. Fleur's face floats in front of me. I feel the punch in my gut, rising up and exploding in tears and screaming, and the pain is so intense that I don't even know where I am anymore. My only desire, strong as instinct, is not to exist.

Fleur is dead.

"No," I say out loud. "She's not dead. She wasn't sick. She'd gotten really involved in the nights, but she was doing fine. My Fleur."

She didn't think she was lost. Was she? Why didn't I sense it? Why didn't I do anything? I never tried to figure out a reason for her absences, those long stretches when I didn't hear from her. I just thought, *Oh, that's just how it is; that's how these night-people are. They lose track of time, but sooner or later they pop up again. Fleur isn't forgetting about me.* But I . . . I forgot about her, for fear I would get lost again in my passion for the night.

"It was a whole thing with the drug squad," Poppy says. "They came here. Can you believe it, Rose?"

Fleur, dead from having forgotten that she was holding on to life, from having desired a perfect world, from getting too upset when things weren't just so. Dead from wanting to live in that uncomfortable zone where desire risks burning too hot, burning itself out. Dead from indifference. *I don't care,* she said, and men swarmed between her thighs, and women, too. She didn't want children. What point is there in giving life when it always ends in death?

Grief surges and breaks over me like a tidal wave, and I am nothing, nowhere, and it lashes me inside and outside and, like a slap, I see Fleur's smile, her real one, the one she wore when she opened the door and, just from that smile, I knew she had conquests to tell me about. She told me intimate little details about her lovers' bodies, their little flaws, the tongue they slipped into her mouth, the closeness, the sweet words, the disgusting things.

Sitting in the dressing room, I stare at her locker. Under her name, she'd drawn a flower and stuck a photo of the two of us. I didn't know that photo was here.

Andrea approaches, strokes my cheek.

No words. There are no words for this.

She hands me the large pair of wire-cutters I've seen her use occasionally in the past, when a girl didn't show up or get in touch for at least six months. That girl's locker had to be opened and emptied, so someone else could use it. Tonight, she's given me the job of opening Fleur's locker.

"We wanted to open it with you," Poppy says, still hiccupping with sobs. "There might be some of her stuff still inside, and we could share it, don't you think?"

The padlock gives a dry snap as it breaks, and the locker opens. Mascara, nail polish, tweezers in an open makeup kit. A few stockings hang from a little rod. Her stage outfits are in a black velvet bag. I empty the bag's contents onto a table in a cascade of sequined fabric, garters, bras. Fleur's perfume rises from the pile of clothing like a gust of cold wind, blurred memories stinging my face. It's too hard.

Poppy pulls Fleur's favorite dress out of the pile, a sparkling thing with a plunging neckline.

"This one is for you, Rose."

She knows I love that dress. I went starry-eyed whenever Fleur wore it. Fleur, a music-box ballerina in her little case of light. Fleur, an ethereal femme fatale, distant and lascivious. When she appeared on the stage, it was like a sudden eruption of flame, a magic trick, cries of wonder swirling around her. I press the dress to my nostrils, wanting to suffocate myself on the perfume that wafts from it. I feel as if her body is there, physically, in her scent, and the pain lessens. I want to wear it. I take off my clothes and slip it on as Poppy takes possession of a red dress, Iris a black one. Rebecca tries on a bra.

Mélisse hands me a pair of heels.

"I want you to wear something of mine, too. Take these heels, I want you to have them."

Poppy opens her locker and takes out a small box.

"These'll look great on you," she says. "False eyelashes, brand new."

It was Poppy who made me up on my first night here. The memory is so vivid, like it happened yesterday. I sit down in the same spot in front of the mirror and let Poppy work on me. She deploys the false lashes, and glue, makeup brushes, blush, lipstick, and then makes herself up, too, next to me. At last she smiles, takes my face in her hands, pressing her lips to my lips and leaving a trace of her smile on my mouth. Thank you, Poppy, so young and so strong.

Now Iris comes near and gives me a pretty black velvet ribbon, which I tie around my neck. Andrea does my hair, adding some life to it with a curling iron. Rebecca gives me a new garter, very delicate, the way I like them. I try on the heels Mélisse gave me, and it comes back in an instant, the desire to sway my hips. I look at my legs in the big mirror, and then I go upstairs, to the main room, to find Fleur. She is there, at the bar. I can see her ordering her first drink, a gin fizz or a vodka tonic. Her scarlet lips gleam. Fleur drinks, crosses her legs, her garter glittering in my tear-filled eyes. She dances with the night, a dark light among dark lights. We often used to leave together after work. She'd text to make sure I got home safely. "Write me," she would say, and I would write, "Are you home yet, my Fleur? I'm home." "I took the bus," she would write back. "Couldn't get a taxi and all the better, because this way it's free. I've got this, babe."

Fleur didn't always go home. I knew that.

Other times we'd walk down the Champs, holding hands. Sometimes she would dance, fluttering like a butterfly around me while I just gazed at her, captivated. I didn't understand her joy, all that energy she had, enough to dance like a butterfly in the street at five o'clock in the morning. But I would grasp her hand and feel as if my heart were about to explode, that all this intoxication would last forever.

I liked asking her, "What will you do after all this? Do you have plans for the future?" She never wanted to answer, just shrugged her shoulders and kept dancing, like a child lost in daydreams, somewhere up in the clouds. Once, just once, she deigned to give me a reply.

"This is all I really love, you know. It's incredible to be onstage, to dance almost nude, to wear clothes you'd never wear otherwise. Life after this is just ugliness, because you turn normal."

Fleur, my Fleur, you will never turn normal, never leave the night, the crazy life, the wild laughter and your intoxications. You'll dance naked forever.

Poppy comes up beside me and says in my ear, "Fleur's with us. I know she's glad, up there, that you're here with us, wearing her dress." She's handing me her glass just as the DJ's velvety voice announces the next girl onstage. I jerk awake, there, deep in the heart of the night: *Rose Lee, next*. Rose Lee, that's me. Poppy keeps her hold on the glass and is about to nudge me in the direction of the stage, but my feet, my legs, my chest, my whole body is already heading for the transparent surface of the platform. I do it, drawn by the irresistible desire to move, to let the sadness fly away with the notes of the music, and it sings inside me, it sings on this stage where I am gliding on my own sorrowful thoughts. *The heart is a bloom . . . Shoots up through the stony ground . . . it's a beautiful day . . . Sky falls . . . it's a beautiful day . . . Don't let it get away . . .* I love this song by U2, and the DJ knows it. The girls come near the stage, call the customers, stubbornly determined to banish their grief with elation. I want to dance with them. They and I are a single female body flooded with overwhelming emotion, too much to carry without the help of the stage lights. Poppy wraps her arms around me, Mélisse rests one hand on my ass while the other caresses my cheek, Iris kisses me on the lips. Being here, on this stage, sweeps away the fear, erases the pain.

Rebecca steps onstage with us, too. I can see it now, she's lost forever the air of being a nice little girl. Her gaze is serious, powerful. She has dyed her hair strawberry blonde. I watch her dance; her movements have become smooth and supple, she has learned sensuality the way you catch a disease. She has it now, and she'll have it forever.

We form a circle, Poppy in the middle. She slips off her dress, curves her back forward to make her breasts droop, clenches her buttocks so the cellulite stands out. She plays at making herself ugly, sinking into the joke to mimic homeliness and fatness, her body flaccid, her skin sagging, a hideous grimace on her face. She waddles like a duck, my beautiful Poppy, and I burst out laughing, because she is talented, without shame, laughing and making others laugh. Now our tears are from laughing too hard, and we are radiant, and one . . . two . . . three . . . we all take off our bras at the same moment and shimmy our shoulders, fast, faster, to make our breasts jiggle, side to side, up and down. Rebecca helps hers along with her hands; the fake ones won't move by themselves. Poppy looks over at Andrea, who is standing near the bar, watching us. She has abandoned her role as censor tonight; her face is gentle. She smiles, and I know she is moved. She nods *yes* to Poppy. Men are approaching the stage now, timidly, a few hands outstretched, holding money. But we almost don't even see them anymore, all these astonished customers who are surely thinking, *Where the hell are we? What's going on?*; we don't reach for the money they toss at our feet. We are completely naked, but it's only for ourselves and no one else; we've shed our vanity, we're lighter for having wept tears black with mascara, and this is a sublime moment, perfect. Death, no, we do not acquiesce; that's why, dangerously, we're dancing without any clothes on now, even our G-strings have joined the pile of stage outfits we have tossed all around us, on tables and chairs. Poppy grasps the pole, a firm, solid line stretching away in a vertical horizon to which she clings and climbs, higher and higher, up to the ceiling. Every eye in the room follows her as she flips upside-down, legs bent, grip sure, and descends slowly, turning around and around the pole. She is an acrobat, a whirlwind. She slows down and then speeds up, and her body is the central axis of the perpetual movement of a star. We watch her, like the dream of a summer night.

Epilogue

Everything is clear, coming back like the memory of childhood, the taste of grandmother's cooking, the scent of eau de Cologne, something intangible and yet indelible. I haven't forgotten a single moment of what I experienced. Everything is the way it was before, though it all feels different without Fleur. But that's what I want to remember the most. I'd fled the night, certain that in it lurked the ultimate offense, the risk of erasing what I'd learned elsewhere with so much effort. Sometimes it was like I could see all the books, filing past in front of me, that I'd absorbed and regurgitated with discipline, the degrees earned, the joys of the intellect, the love of knowledge, Pascal's wager, the Soul, God, Beauty. Hadrien, too, had seemed like a very good reason to stop. But in the face of this clarity, another certainty, fierce and unalterable, took up residence inside me. The certainty that, weighed down with all my bookish knowledge, I had been living in ignorance. Ignorant of real experience, of deep emotion, of understanding of the human condition and of myself. Especially of myself. Before being anyone at all, I should have been Rose Lee.

I want to be Rose Lee. Queen or whore, it doesn't matter, when the happiest moments of my life are spent here, nude, wearing the false eyelashes Poppy gave me.